reckless

it girl novels created by Cecily von Ziegesar:

It Girl
Notorious
Reckless

If you like **the it girl**, you may also enjoy:

Bass Ackwards and Belly Up by Elizabeth Craft and Sarah Fain

Secrets of My Hollywood Life by Jen Calonita

Haters by Alisa Valdes-Rodriguez

reckless

an it girl novel

CREATED BY
CECILY VON ZIEGESAR

LB 1837
LITTLE, BROWN AND COMPANY
New York Boston

Copyright © 2006 by Alloy Entertainment

All rights reserved.

Little, Brown and Company
1271 Avenue of the Americas, New York, NY 10020
Visit our Web site at www.lb-teens.com

First Edition: November 2006

The characters and events in this book are fictitious. Any similarity to real persons, living or dead, is coincidental and not intended by the author.

Produced by Alloy Entertainment
151 West 26th Street, New York, NY 10001

ON THE COVER: dress—ABS by Allen Schwartz,
earrings & necklace—Yvette Fry Inc.

ISBN-10: 0-316-01187-8
ISBN-13: 978-0-316-01187-7

10 9 8 7 6 5 4 3 2 1
CWO
Printed in the United States of America

Oh what a tangled web we weave, when first we practice to deceive!

—Sir Walter Scott

WAVERLY OWLS DO NOT KISS BOYS IN PUBLIC.

A cold, gray rain splattered against the huge plate glass windows of the art studio. Instead of focusing on the enormous sheet of newsprint sprawled on the desk in front of her, Jenny Humphrey found herself thinking about the love scene from *Match Point* where Jonathan Rhys Meyers practically devours Scarlett Johansson's head with his mouth out in the field in the pouring rain. Of course, if she had *her* way, it would be sexy Waverly Academy junior Easy Walsh devouring her head. (And like in the movie, it would be summer in the English countryside and not an ice-cold autumn day in upstate New York.) Sexy Waverly Academy junior Easy Walsh—who just happened to be her boyfriend.

Last week, frizzy-haired Mrs. Silver had invited Jenny, Easy, and Alison Quentin to join her Wednesday afternoon Human Figure Drawing elective. She'd pulled them aside after their portraiture class and with a proud voice and a glint in her crinkly blue eyes said, "You are my stars." By joining the Human Figure Drawing class, she'd reasoned, they'd be able to get a better understanding of the body and enhance their already-impressive talents. Jenny had been thrilled—it was totally flattering to be taken aside after only a few weeks of class and told that she was talented. And the thought of getting to spend a little extra time with Easy didn't hurt, either.

When she arrived at the studio after lunch, Jenny took a seat near the door. In the center of the room was a large platform about a foot off the ground with a single chair on it. The desks were arranged around the platform in a semicircle. Her eyes scanned the class, hoping for a glimpse of Easy's adorable head of curly dark brown hair. She recognized a few people. Parker DuBois, the senior from France (or was it Belgium?) that the girls were always whispering about, a tall Indian girl from her field hockey team, a girl she and Brett had taken to calling the Girl in Black. Finally she spotted Easy way over by the supply closets. He'd been staring at her while she scoped out the class and gave her a little wave, making her heart flutter. Not that it wasn't already fluttering.

When Jenny wasn't daydreaming out the rainy window, she found the two-hour class to be wonderfully challenging. Every five minutes Mrs. Silver asked a different student to go up and pose as directed. Fully clothed, of course, so it really wasn't anything to be embarrassed about, although Jenny didn't like the idea of the whole class drawing her giant boobs. Luckily, she wasn't called up. But Easy was. Mrs. Silver had him sit in the chair and tie his shoes, and Jenny couldn't help thinking how much better her drawing would be if he had his shirt off. Before class ended, Mrs. Silver circled the room and selected the very best sketches of the day (Easy's, Parker's, and Girl in Black's) for Friday's student gallery show, which not so accidentally coincided with Waverly's Trustee Weekend.

By the time the students were dismissed, the wind had picked up and it looked like an all-out monsoon outside. Good thing she was wearing her Jeffery Campbell rubber rain boots with their funky, multicolored floral design. Cute, yes—but functional, too. She'd read in *Real Simple* magazine on a rainy afternoon spent paging through the periodicals in Waverly's library (instead of memorizing Latin conjugations) that it was helpful to the psyche to wear something bright and colorful on dreary, wet days. Jenny had taken the advice to heart and used it as an excuse to buy the rubber boots and an adorable red vinyl Benetton trench coat that she'd found online—it was a kids size and a little tight around the chest, but wearing it made her feel like smiling.

Not that she needed *another* reason.

Jenny stood up and removed the straps of her schoolbag from the back of her chair. "Drop something?" she heard a low voice behind her say as something poked her gently in the back. She whirled around, and there was Easy, brandishing her pale pink umbrella like a fencing sword.

"You don't want to borrow it?" she offered, stepping aside to let the rest of the class escape.

"Not exactly my color." Easy dropped his canvas messenger

bag to the floor and slipped on his maroon Waverly blazer. The Waverly handbook, which Jenny had studied religiously before arriving at boarding school until realizing no one took it seriously at all, stated that all Waverly blazers had to be in an "appropriately maintained" condition. Whatever that meant. Jenny was sure Easy's blazer, with its half-peeled-off crest, frayed cuffs, and permanent wrinkles, wouldn't make the cut.

"Don't be so sure. You look nice in maroon, and that's just a couple of shades away from pink on Mrs. Silver's color wheel," she joked, taking her umbrella from him.

He leaned toward her conspiratorially. "You look nice in every color."

Jenny coughed to disguise the dopey grin she felt creeping across her face.

"And," Easy continued, "you look especially hot with charcoal gray on your cheeks." He placed his hand on the small of her back and led her out of the studio.

"What?" Jenny peered at her reflection in one of the sculpture display cases lining the hallway. There was a splotchy gray shadow on her right cheek. Ack! There she was, thinking how romantic it would be if she was alone in the art studio with Easy, and the whole time he was wondering when she was going to notice the dirt on her face. Jenny quickly grabbed a tissue from the pocket of her jeans and dabbed at her cheeks. She needed some water but wasn't about to spit in front of Easy. Gross. She shrugged and stepped boldly through the main doors into the stormy afternoon. "The rain will wash it off."

She shook open her umbrella and held it over both their heads as they descended the stairs of the art building. "Where are you off to?" Jenny asked, walking on her tiptoes to give Easy a little more headroom. Even though Jenny could already feel her hair frizzing in the dampness, she could appreciate the beauty of the chilly, drizzling rain. The Waverly quad still managed to look stunning—the grass looked unnaturally green, and the brilliant reds and oranges of the enormous oak trees were all cloaked in a lovely gray mist. It looked like a postcard. And she lived in it.

Easy patted the front pocket of his brown-and-white-striped T-shirt from Abercrombie & Fitch. It was so gauzy, it would probably disintegrate the next time it went through the wash. Jenny fought the urge to run her hands up and down his chest—to feel the shirt, of course. "I'd better head over to the stables and check on Credo. She gets a little freaked out by the rain."

"Give her a carrot for me." The day she met Credo had been the first time Jenny ever rode a horse—or kissed Easy Walsh. Time seemed to fly at Waverly. About a week and a half had gone by since Easy came back early from Tinsley Carmichael's Café Society party in Boston and snuck Jenny out to the bluffs to watch the sunrise. They'd talked, and kissed, and held each other. It was . . . heavenly. It was one of those things you don't quite expect to ever happen to you or, at least, not if you're short, curly-haired, giant-boobed sophomore Jenny Humphrey.

Easy smiled down at Jenny and kicked at one of the flood-lights set to light up the carved swirling topiaries that lined the building's edge. "You could come with me," he suggested, a sheepish look crossing his face, as if he was thinking about giving someone other than Credo a nice, long rubdown.

Jenny twirled the umbrella playfully over their heads. Another rainy afternoon trapped inside the stables with Easy—alone? Sounded a little too tempting. She shook her head slowly. "You know I'd love to, but it's probably not the best idea. I've got a giant English paper due on Friday, and I should really spend some quality time with my laptop in the library."

She didn't want to sound like a tool, but she was getting good grades here and wanted to keep it up. Jenny rested her umbrella-free hand on Easy's wrist; the contact with his skin gave her a rush that surpassed what she'd felt when she scored her first goal in last week's game against Briarwood Academy. Wait, she was turning him down to *study*? Was she insane?

"I guess I can wait," Easy drawled in his adorable Kentucky accent. "If you insist." His dark blue eyes met Jenny's, and chills ran down her spine all the way to the toes of her perky rubber boots.

"We'll do something really fun this weekend," Jenny promised as they made their way along the gravel path toward Dumbarton. "We'll go riding on Friday and then grab some dinner after. Maybe I'll try a canter?"

Easy grinned. "Excellent. I'll tell Credo you're up for a challenge this time."

"No!" Jenny cried, bumping her hip against Easy and sending him out from under her umbrella and into the storm. "Last time was challenging enough."

Easy dove back underneath the umbrella and snaked his arm through hers. "I'll walk you back to your room, then?"

Just the mention of the word *room* made her stiffen. Part, or actually most, of the reason for Jenny's newfound studiousness was because she was terrified of being alone with her roommate, Callie Vernon. Even the stuffy old library seemed like a cheerful alternative.

Jenny used to live in a quad with Callie, Tinsley, and Brett Messerschmidt. But after Tinsley and Callie were caught sneaking back to Waverly after their presidential suite party at the Boston Ritz-Bradley, Dean Marymount split the girls up. The first week after Brett and Tinsley moved downstairs from Dumbarton 303 to Dumbarton 121 was the most uncomfortable one of Jenny's life—worse even than the time she'd gotten her period on a camping trip with her father in the wilds of Vermont and she'd had to wear the ancient diaper-like pads they'd sold at the nearest general store. Callie had this humiliating way of looking straight past Jenny, not even like she was ignoring her, but like she didn't even exist. It was probably the only way Callie could deal with the fact that her new roommate had captured her boyfriend's heart. Whether or not Jenny had done it on purpose was of no consequence to Callie. She *had* done it.

One evening, Jenny came home from the library to find Callie stuffing her freshly laundered clothes into her closet. (All the really rich kids sent their laundry out to the local Fluff 'n' Fold. Jenny felt like a total plebian for using the coin-run machines in the basement.) She noticed that Callie's long, normally wild strawberry blond locks had been chopped to just below her shoulders and sleekly layered. After much debate, Jenny finally said, "Wow, your hair looks fabulous!" and totally meant it. But Callie only yawned and checked her teeth for lipstick stains in the mirror.

The only time Callie had spoken to her since the Boston weekend had been unpleasant, to put it politely. "Is that a new dress?" Jenny had asked one afternoon, expecting no response as usual. After all, the question was pointless. Ever since the breakup with Easy, *all* of Callie's clothes were new. Crumpled packages from Saks and Barneys and Anthropologie piled higher in the trash every day, and shoe boxes from Missoni and Michael Kors were starting to stack up, unopened, by Callie's closet door. Callie spun around, her new hair falling into place as if it had been born that way, and said regally, "Yes. And if there was any chance of it fitting you, I'd be concerned about you stealing *it*," before stomping out of the room, leaving Jenny's mouth hanging open.

And so she had gone out of her way to give Callie the space she needed, making it a habit to wake up early, shower, get dressed, and escape, all before Callie even took off her purple silk eye mask and climbed out of bed. It was an exhausting, shadowy way to live, and Jenny was getting tired of having to always figure out when Callie would be out of the room so that she could sneak back in.

"You okay?" Easy raised the collar of his blazer to shield himself from the driving rain. Water was pooling on top of his Doc Martens of indeterminate color—black? Oxblood? Dirt-covered?

One frayed yellow lace hung loose and trailed behind him, already muddy, as he shuffled his feet against the gravel pebbles of the walkway with his toe. Even his shoes were cute.

"I guess I am." Jenny suddenly dropped her umbrella to the grass beside the path and raised her face to the rainy sky, letting the cool drops splash onto her skin. She missed New York, just a little. Her new rubber boots would be perfect for splashing around in the puddles that must be forming right now in front of her building on West End Avenue and 99th Street.

Easy didn't seem to mind the impromptu shower. He stepped closer, and when she turned her face toward him, she saw his eyes sparkling with the rain, a dripping dark brown curl plastered to his forehead. "You are so goddamned cute." He leaned down and gently nuzzled his wet nose against hers before kissing her.

Truth was, if she had to see another girl with Easy, she'd hate her too. She didn't blame Callie. Despite her gorgeous new haircut and trendy new outfits, Callie was still hurting. But Jenny couldn't help it. Easy was amazing, and if she had to give up her friendship with Callie to be with him, so be it. He was totally worth it.

"You're ringing," Jenny muttered softly, pulling away from Easy as she felt his phone vibrate in his blazer pocket.

"I didn't hear anything." Easy grinned, putting both hands on Jenny's waist and pulling her back toward him.

"What if it's important?"

"More important than this?" he murmured. "Impossible!"

They stayed like that, kissing in the rain in front of

Dumbarton for a long time. Jenny stood on the lowest step and still had to raise her chin a little to meet Easy's gaze. And for the millionth time, she chased away the thought of how much easier it must have been for Callie to kiss him—she was about seven inches taller than Jenny.

But if she was having this much trouble not thinking about Callie and Easy and she was the one *with* him, poor Callie must be really tortured. Or maybe it was better to have had Easy once and then lost him than to never have had him at all. Jenny wasn't so sure. She certainly didn't want to find out.

Instant Message Inbox

AlanStGirard: Just saw Marymount having a pretty intense cup of tea with Miss Rose at CoffeeRoasters—she the babe you caught him banging at the Ritz?

TinsleyCarmichael: So eloquent you are. But no.

AlanStGirard: Why won't you tell, gdamn it?

TinsleyCarmichael: Bcuz secrets are worth more than gossip, dummy. And I have a feeling that info could come in handy sometime.

AlanStGirard: You got any dirt on me?

TinsleyCarmichael: Ha. If you only knew . . . Just stay on my good side, ASG.

A WAVERLY OWL TAKES ADVANTAGE OF FORTUITOUS EVENTS.

"Hey, Princess," Heath Ferro shouted as he flung open the door to the second-floor Richards dorm room he shared with Brandon Buchanan, his navy blue vintage Pumas soaked and squeaking noisily against the previously clean blond oak floor. "Aw," he cooed when he saw the drawn curtains and Brandon curled up beneath his extremely prissy, peach-colored chenille throw. "Is Sleeping Beauty *still* sleeping?"

Asshole, Brandon cursed into his pillow. Maybe a person with a normal degree of self-awareness could walk into a room, notice the closed curtains, the Hammacher Schlemmer Sound Oasis machine tuned to "Summer Night," the body under the covers and think, *Maybe I* won't *stomp around like a moron*. Apparently that was too much to ask of Heath.

"Fuck off, Ferro," Brandon growled as he raised his head

from his pillow high enough to give Heath a withering glare. The problem with Heath—or *one* problem with Heath—was that he was too self-absorbed to give a shit whether or not his roommate was sleeping or studying or wallowing in self-pity. Heath came in only one volume: loud.

"Don't you have practice, dude?" Heath flicked on the light switch, and the darkened lair was flooded with fluorescent light. Brandon pulled the blanket up over his face.

Practice. Yeah, he had practice. And since he was junior captain of the squash team, he should probably get off his ass and show up. But the thought of smacking a stupid rubber ball around a fifteen-by-fifteen room with another sweaty guy—well, he just wasn't up for it today. Brandon had uncharacteristically skipped his last class of the day—the gray rainy day depressed him and made him want nothing more than to curl up in his cozy bed, take a long nap, and maybe never wake up.

That was a little morbid, yeah. But he hadn't been feeling himself since the weekend before last, when Callie Vernon had completely humiliated him by ordering him to watch some gay porno in front of everyone at the Ritz-Bradley party. Sure, he'd been acting a little overprotective—but Callie was making a total ass of herself, jumping up on the desk and drunkenly tearing off her clothes to try and keep up with Tinsley. It always made Brandon sick to think about how little self-respect Callie had and how highly she esteemed the quite possibly sociopathic Tinsley. He couldn't help it—it killed him to see her acting like a mindless clone. He had asked her to come back to his room to talk in private. Or maybe do a little more than just talk. But Callie had mocked him, screaming at him to leave her alone.

Well, if that's the way she wanted it, fine. He was tired of obsessing over Callie. Besides, she was clearly not over artsy-fartsy Easy Walsh. He could tell the sole reason she'd gotten up on that dresser to do her little striptease was she'd caught Easy admiring Tinsley's body and it killed her. He found both Tinsley and Easy loathsome—and of course, Callie idolized both of them. He wasn't about to wait around for her to realize what soulless slimebags they were and come running back to him.

If only he had something better to do . . .

Brandon tossed off his ultra-soft blanket and set his bare feet on the cold wooden floor. He was already dressed for practice in his navy blue Adidas track pants with the orange stripes down the sides and one of the white Lacoste jersey tees that he bought by the dozen—he liked to wear them to practice, but once the armpits got sweat stains, he threw them out. "Don't get your panties in a bunch, Ferro. I was just taking a quick catnap."

"You said 'panties' and 'catnap' in the same sentence!!" Heath laughed maniacally as he pulled off his rain-soaked white Diesel men's T-shirt with the words IN A MORAL PANIC emblazoned across the front, balled it up, and tossed it at Brandon's head. It missed and landed in a soggy heap on Brandon's desk. Nice. It was hard to imagine Heath's morals in a panic—he didn't have any.

Brandon crossed the room to his dresser, sighing as he stepped over the mucky footprints Heath had left behind, and pulled a pair of neatly rolled white Adidas gym socks from a drawer. His biting response to Heath was cut off indefinitely by the jangling of his black Treo on his oak bedside table.

Callie? Brandon flipped it open to see his father's number. Suppressing a groan, he answered. "Good afternoon, Father."

"You sound sleepy." Mr. Buchanan's sonorous voice contained a touch of accusation. "I hope I didn't wake you. Though why you would you be napping in the middle of a school day, I can't imagine."

Great. He was sounding even more passive-aggressive than normal. Must be his mega-bitch twenty-something gold digger wife rubbing off on him. "I was getting ready for practice. Is something wrong?" Mr. Buchanan was a weary man, older than his years—but Brandon guessed that's what came from starting a new family when you're already a legal senior citizen. Brandon's bratty twin half brothers, Zachary and Luke, were more annoying than Tom Cruise on speed. No wonder his dad worked so much.

Mr. Buchanan ignored his son's question or didn't hear it. "I'm having dinner with Dean Marymount this Friday. I'd like you to come. Bring Callie."

Dean Marymount? Callie? What the fuck was his dad talking about? "You're coming . . . here?" Brandon asked, confused.

Mr. Buchanan sighed, and Brandon could hear train noises in the background. He must be on his commute to Greenwich from the city. "Brandon, I hope you pay better attention to your studies than you do to your father. I have trustee meetings at Waverly all weekend. I told you about it months ago."

"Trustee Weekend," Brandon repeated. "Sorry, it slipped

my mind," he added, although he knew his father had never mentioned it. Always better to take blame himself than expect his father to admit fault. But fuck—dinner with Dean Marymount? Did he really deserve that kind of punishment? And Callie? Guess he wasn't the only forgetful one. "Um . . . maybe it slipped your mind that I broke up with Callie? About a year ago?"

"You never tell me anything," Mr. Buchanan grumbled after a pause. "Fine, then. Bring someone else. I don't want it to be just the three of us. That would be . . . rather dull, don't you agree?"

You think?

"Yeah, okay, I'll bring someone." Parents were such freaks. "Look, Dad, I've got practice."

"All right, I hope you win. Make reservations for eight at that place—the French one." Mr. Buchanan clicked off before Brandon could repeat that it was practice, not a game. You don't win at practice.

"Did you really say the magic words?" Heath asked the second Brandon tossed his phone into his black nylon squash bag. Heath was grinning like a five-year-old who'd just heard the jingle of the ice cream truck.

"Huh?"

"*Trustee Weekend,*" Heath repeated, the rapturous expression spreading across his face. He still hadn't put on a shirt and was standing in the middle of the room in just a short pair of red Nike soccer shorts covered in grass stains. "You know what that means."

"Yeah. A bunch of self-important rich fogies come to town and make their poor, overworked sons eat frogs legs at Le Petit Cock with the fucking dean. It means torture."

"No, moron," Heath interrupted, grabbing a soccer ball and bouncing it expertly on his knee. "It means a bunch of self-important rich fogies come to town, and everyone's so fucking busy falling over backward to keep them happy that they don't even notice what the fucking smarter-than-they-think students are doing. And that"—Heath grinned—"means paaar-TAY!" He punctuated this by kicking the ball at Brandon's bookshelf and sending the contents of the top shelf sliding to the floor.

Brandon rolled his eyes. Heath had been kind of impossible since the Boston weekend, when Tinsley's secret society made the brilliant decision to make Heath its next male target. Like his giant ego could get any more inflated. Brandon had left the party early, after Callie had humiliatingly chastised him in front of everyone, but he'd heard rumors about what had happened afterward. Supposedly Callie, Tinsley, and Heath had climbed up to the roof and danced around naked? But no one seemed to know for sure. All they knew was that when they woke up hung over and half dressed on the hotel suite floor in the morning, the three of them were gone. It sounded *très* suspicious to Brandon, but he and Callie weren't exactly in speaking mode—and the last thing on earth he wanted to hear was that she'd actually done something as stupid as sleep with Heath Ferro.

Because she wouldn't have, right?

Heath grabbed his BlackBerry and pressed a button on his

speed dial. "Trying to find a date for the weekend already?" Brandon quipped, pulling on his bright yellow waterproof windbreaker. Actually, he was the one who needed a date. Who the hell was he going to ask to come to dinner with his dad and Dean Marymount?

"As if," Heath scoffed. "I'm calling my buddy at Rhinecliff Liquors. What's a party without refreshments?"

Instant Message Inbox

SageFrancis: Has Smail called off practice yet?

BennyCunningham: Just checked my email . . . we're meeting at Lasell instead, 4 sharp.

SageFrancis: Dibs on the Stairmaster with the best view of the soccer hotties stretching!

BennyCunningham: I don't know how the sweaty narsty gym can turn you on. . . .

SageFrancis: That's because you've never made out in a shower stall in the boys' locker room.

BennyCunningham: Oh, yeah? w/who?

SageFrancis: Guess you're going to have to wait for another game of T or D to find out.

A WAVERLY OWL DOES NOT RUMMAGE IN HER ROOMMATE'S BELONGINGS— SHE MIGHT FIND SOMETHING.

Rainy days always made Callie Vernon unbearably drowsy, and she could barely keep her eyes open during AP American History, something Mr. Wilde, the bookish thirty-something professor, seemed not to notice. Normally, his deep baritone voice and always slightly crooked smile were enough to keep Callie's attention, but not when 2 P.M. looked like 9 P.M.—it was a fucking monsoon out there. Field hockey practice had been canceled, which sounded nice but wasn't actually a treat in any sense of the word. Canceled practice meant everyone had to report to Lasell, the out-of-date fitness center, and spend an hour on the cardio machines, which Callie loathed. No matter how skinny she wanted to be, she couldn't bear walking in place while everyone cooed at the boys jogging in the gym through the glass. Besides, Lasell smelled like feet.

And on a rainy day like this, all the other teams would have canceled practice too, and the gym would be full of hot, sweaty, stinky boys.

Mr. Wilde dismissed the class. Callie, rapidly blinking to shake the sleep out of herself, passed him in the doorway; he smiled his crooked smile. "Looks like you could use a nap." That counted as teacher permission to skip practice, didn't it? Or at least show up late?

And so, an hour later, when Callie woke up from her afternoon *siesta*, a word her mother had taught her to use instead of *nap* (as the latter brought with it a lazy connotation), she yawned and hopped out of bed, wearing only her Calvin Klein French-cut black underwear and matching stretchy camisole. She could walk around naked if she wanted since she practically had a single now. Ever since Tinsley and Brett had moved out, she barely saw Jenny anymore. Callie woke up every morning to an empty room and crawled into bed after her nightly Pilates routine, the whole day having often gone by without her seeing her busty little roomie. And that's exactly the way she wanted it.

She might have been suspicious that Jenny was sleeping somewhere else—a thought that would have driven her mad with jealousy, as if little Jenny Humphrey could manage to sneak into the boys' dorm every night and have wild, passionate, illicit sex with Easy Walsh. But thankfully, every morning the ginseng-honey scent of Jenny's Frederic Fekkai Curl Enhancing Lotion hung in the air assured Callie that her little pest of a boyfriend-stealing roommate was actually sleeping in her own bed. Or maybe she was just a super-early riser.

Jenny really seemed to be afraid of her. As well she should be.

Not that Callie's life wasn't better without Easy Walsh. Since they'd broken up (she'd convinced herself that it was mutual and that she had not actually been dumped on her skinny ass), Callie had managed to snag an A on her last bio test, score six goals in the last two field hockey games, and flirt with just about every single cute guy on campus. Last Thursday, she had received special permission to take the train into Manhattan for a "medical emergency" and had spent the afternoon at Bergdorf-Goodman followed by six sample sales in the Garment District. Walking off the train at Rhinecliff station, arms loaded with bags of Theory clothes (trunk show!), wearing new Christian Louboutin platform espadrilles with sexy ankle ties and adorable butterflies embroidered on the toes, her newly cut, fresh-from-the-Red-Door-Salon-smelling blond locks six inches shorter and swooshing against her shoulders, she felt . . . lighter. And free! Although she'd feel a whole lot lighter if Easy wasn't dating her roommate. Or better yet, if he wasn't dating anyone at all.

Callie glanced at herself in her dresser mirror and shook her head, enjoying the way her new haircut looked in motion. She bet Easy would like it.

Fuck. It was so hard to turn off feelings that had been alive and pulsing for over a year. Just because Easy suddenly decided he was better off with a silly little pink-cheeked sophomore with stripper-sized breasts, she was supposed to just get over it? It was hard. For twelve months, Easy had been the one in her thoughts as she crawled into bed at night. When she saw a pretty white wedding gown in a magazine, it was Easy she dreamed of wearing it for. She sighed. She would take him back in half a second.

Callie felt her cheeks heating up. Tinsley was the only one she could still talk to about how hurt she was over the whole breakup. Instead of getting bored with it, Tinsley seemed to enjoy hearing about it. She almost seemed more pissed off at Jenny than Callie was.

Outside, the rain seemed to have slowed a bit. Callie yawned once again and decided to get her shit together and get on over to the gym. Exercise released endorphins, the only all-natural antidepressants. If she couldn't get her hands on any of her mom's Paxil, she might as well hop on a treadmill. From her overstuffed top dresser drawer (the one dedicated to her gym clothes, field hockey uniforms, and other fugly things), Callie pulled out a pair of stone-colored Adidas by Stella McCartney gym pants and stepped into them.

Hair band, hair band, Callie thought as she glanced over her dresser top. She was always losing them. Where the fuck did they all go? Guiltily she glanced at Jenny's dresser. It was almost as messy as hers. Maybe if Jenny hadn't turned out to be such a scheming, backstabbing boyfriend stealer, they might have become friends.

Without hesitation, Callie strode over to Jenny's dresser and reached for her Altoids tin full of hair bands. Her hand paused in midair, however, when she spotted the folded piece of notebook paper with the letter *J* on it. She touched the letter and it smeared. Charcoal.

Her heartbeat increased tenfold. She snatched up the piece of paper and examined Easy's familiar, eight-year-old penmanship—only he could make the letter *J* look practically illegible. She paused for a moment to debate the moral implications of reading someone else's private note before her curiosity got the best of her.

On the inside of the paper there were no words, just a drawing, in pencil. It was a caricature of a guy with a giant head of dark, unruly hair, wearing beat-up jeans with holes in the knees and a T-shirt with a peace sign on it. It was easy to guess who he was supposed to be. Easy. He was blowing a kiss.

Before she knew what she was doing, Callie had crumpled the paper into a tiny, tight ball. She stared at it in her palm for a second before stuffing it into the tiny zip-up pocket in her track pants, meant only for a gym locker key. Her eyes raced around the room, searching for something to break or tear apart or throw against the wall or . . . She spotted the Altoids tin and grabbed a fist full of Jenny's hair bands and flung them one by one, slingshot style, around the room in every direction. Her incredible fury dissipated as each one went flying through the air and disappeared into the piles of crumpled-up designer clothes heaped on the floor.

Grabbing her gym bag, Callie stomped out the door and flew down the two flights of wooden stairs to Tinsley and Brett's room—she desperately needed someone, STAT!, to tell her how much prettier she was than munchkin, top-heavy Jenny and how Easy would regret their breakup for the rest of his life.

But as she sped around the corner, she skidded to a stop. Fuck. Right in front of Tinsley and Brett's door was Jenny, still dressed in slim-fitting ultra-dark jeans tucked into an adorable pair of flowered rain boots and a cute red modish vinyl raincoat. Her dark curly hair was plastered to her forehead, and her pale, perfect skin was slick with water. She might have looked like hell if her cheeks weren't flushed and a cute, self-satisfied smile wasn't perched on her ruby red lips. Her hand was holding a marker and poised to write something on the plastic wipe board hanging on Tinsley's door.

"Oh, hi!" Jenny looked up, startled. "I, uh, was just leaving a note for Brett." Her cheeks colored even more, and Callie just stood there, silent.

Tinsley must have heard them because half a second later, before Callie even had sufficient time to ignore Jenny, the door opened. Tinsley stood there, in just a pair of black yoga pants and matching sports bra. She took in the scene objectively, first giving Callie a quick grin and then focusing her violet eyes on Jenny, who had taken a startled step back, still holding an open red marker in her hand. Tinsley cocked her head, as if trying to imagine what Jenny could be doing at her door.

Jenny practically melted beneath the silence and the withering gazes of the two older girls. "Uh, see you at the gym, I guess. . . ." Her tiny voice trailed off as she backed away toward the stairs.

"Is that my marker?" Tinsley demanded coolly.

"Oh, sorry." Jenny retraced her steps and handed the marker to Tinsley, pulling her hand back as if she was afraid of getting burned. “Can you tell Brett . . . Never mind,” she corrected herself, suddenly remembering that Tinsley and Brett weren’t exactly talking either. “I better go.”

Callie and Tinsley stared at her as she disappeared around the corner. Then Tinsley placed her hand on Callie’s long, slim arm. “Don’t worry. She’ll get what’s coming to her.” Tinsley’s mischievous violet eyes sparkled. She was a schemer, and revenge was her favorite kind of fun. It was obvious she already had a plan in the works to “get” Jenny.

But Callie wasn’t amused. The truth was she didn’t want to get Jenny.

She just wanted Easy back where he belonged.

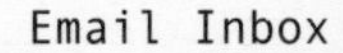

To: BriannaMesserschmidt@elle.com
From: BrettMesserschmidt@waverly.edu
Date: Wednesday, October 2, 4:04 p.m.
Subject: Bliss

Bree,

Haven't heard from you in a while. I hope your boss isn't pulling a *Devil Wears Prada* on you. Things are going well here at good ole Waverly—though I'm planning on being kind of a traitorous Owl this weekend and cheering on St. Lucius's team at Jeremiah's homecoming—but I'll really just be cheering for him. He's been unbelievable lately, and I'm planning on rewarding him soon. . . . I'll keep you posted.

Don't worry, I'll still be your

Little Sis

;)

THE FIELD HOUSE IS AVAILABLE AT SCHEDULED TIMES FOR WAVERLY OWLS TO PRACTICE INDOOR ATHLETICS.

Brett Messerchmidt didn't have time to check her email in between afternoon classes because she hadn't finished the translation of her assigned portion of Ovid's *Metamorphoses* for last-period Latin. She was in an intermediate class, and until three weeks ago, she'd been cursing herself for not testing into beginning Latin, taught by sexy Mr. Dalton. Past tense. Due to an altercation of a sexual kind with a student named Brett, he had been fired and would no longer be available for intimate wine-enhanced student-teacher conferences. Brett was grateful now that her teacher was the somewhat asexual, forty-something Mrs. Graver and not someone she had almost—almost—slept with. Still, the last week and a half with so-in-love-with-her Jeremiah had almost erased all memories of how she'd completely made an ass of herself over Mr. Dalton. Almost.

After class, she grabbed her kelly green Pasha & Jo belted raincoat and rushed out to the field house, hoping to practice shooting before the rest of the field hockey team got there. But there was a note taped on the heavy metal doors, telling the team to meet at Lasell gym instead. Ugh. All the way back across campus in the hair-frizzing rain? Brett tugged on the door—it was unlocked. She grinned and pulled out her phone.

Thirty-five minutes later, she was lying on one of the blue pole-vaulting mats next to Jeremiah. Their bodies sank into the cushy mat like they were sprawled on the softest, queenliest mattress in the world. The field house, where all the Waverly sports teams stored their equipment, felt ghostly and romantic.

"I've never seen the inside of this place." Jeremiah looked up at the high, beamed ceiling, his hands beneath his head. Rain pounded the aluminum roof relentlessly.

Brett turned on her side to face him, grateful that her one-of-a-kind Indian print gypsy skirt was supposed to be crinkled. A short lock of red hair—the piece that always managed to fall into her face no matter how many barrettes she had holding it back—was hanging right in front of her eyes, and it felt like she was looking at Jeremiah through a gauzy red curtain.

Before meeting him, she wasn't into jock types. She was always attracted to older men—well dressed, sophisticated, maybe even European—like Gunther, the Swiss guy she'd met on a ski trip, whom she had supposedly lost her virginity to. At least, that was her story. But now that things were going so well with Jeremiah, she wanted to clear up any lingering misunderstandings between them. When they'd first started dating last year, after meeting at Heath Ferro's spring bash at his parents' estate in Woodstock, she hadn't exactly been up front with him. He'd assumed she was the worldly, mature, experienced girl she'd pretended to be since coming to Waverly. That assumption included the fact (or non-fact) that she wasn't a virgin. She'd made no effort to correct the misunderstanding, even after he'd confided to her that *he* still was. Brett knew it was stupid and immature to pretend to be something she wasn't, but it had made her feel more confident about their relationship. She liked being the one who made the rules, the one who drew the boundaries, the one who had been there, done that. Besides, she hadn't been ready then to tell Jeremiah the truth or to lose her virginity.

But now, things were different.

"You won't get in trouble for skipping practice to make out with your girlfriend?" she asked coyly, tracing her fingers gently across Jeremiah's broad chest. He was so . . . delicious. Brett kept her touch light since, for the whole week following a football game, Jeremiah's entire body was completely bruised and battered. He was St. Lucius's star quarterback this year, and he got tackled a lot.

Speaking of tackling, Brett thought. She rolled toward Jeremiah.

"S'okay." His blue-green eyes swept across her face. "The practice field floods when it rains like this. We're just supposed to put in a few hours at the gym tonight."

"Yeah, I'm supposed to do that too." Brett made a face. "I fucking hate the gym, though. All the goony jock guys—no offense—just drool over the girls in their little Puma shorts. It's kind of gross."

"Wait, you think I'm a jock?" Jeremiah asked in mock surprise.

"You're the star quarterback, sweetheart. Doesn't that automatically make you a jock?" Brett craned her neck and touched his lips with hers, not exactly kissing him. "You're a cute jock, though."

"I guess that's a little better." He kissed her back, a little harder. "And I like it when you call me 'sweetheart.'" It came out *sweet-haht*, in Jeremiah's raw Boston accent. How could she ever have gotten tired of it? It sounded so exotic to her now and even sexier when she thought that this was the way that John F. Kennedy had sounded. Ooh. Kennedys. Jeremiah was practically cut from the same cloth—well, without all the sex and drug scandals. His family was much too sane for that.

"Hey." She pushed his getting-a-little-long reddish brown hair behind his ear. "What are the plans for this weekend?"

"Oh, baby!" Jeremiah moved his hands from his head and rubbed them together over his chest. "It's gonna be awesome. First, we're going to kick Millford's asses at homecoming, then we're going to party like rock-stars." *Rock stahs.*

"Rock stars, huh?" Brett grinned. Sounded like fun. She had been studying hard lately, and it felt good to be thinking about another party. She hadn't been sad to miss the bash at the Ritz-Bradley the other weekend after Tinsley kicked her out of her exclusive girls' club. She'd had much more fun hanging out with Jenny, and, of course, Jeremiah when he snuck into Dumbarton. But ever since the forced room swap, sharing a room exclusively with her former BFF Tinsley Carmichael had caused Brett to do a lot more homework than she normally would. At first, she'd tried to avoid the room as much as possible, spending her evenings in the library, but then she'd realized that meant Tinsley won. And so she started doing her homework in the dorm room with Tinsley, both of them completely ignoring each other. It was slightly fucked up, but Brett wasn't about to cave. After all, Tinsley had stolen Mr. Dalton right out from under her. Sure, it ended up being a blessing in disguise. But deliberately stealing your friend's crush was totally traitorous behavior that deserved a grave punishment.

St. Lucius's homecoming weekend sounded like the perfect opportunity to let loose. "I could get into that."

"Of course you could," Jeremiah agreed. "You'll be the hottest one there."

He was so sweet. She planted another kiss on him. "I guess I'd better start planning my outfit, then." Brett was psyched to get the chance to meet some of Jeremiah's friends. Maybe she could even set Callie up with one of them. Whoa, what was she thinking? *Callie* was barely speaking to her anymore either. Brett had clearly been branded a traitor for being friends with Jenny. Tinsley's friendship she could do without—ever since she'd come back from South Africa that fall, she'd been intolerable. Nastier and even more aloof, if that was possible. But it felt funny not being close to Callie anymore. She missed hearing her babble in her sleep. Sometimes she'd even have whole conversations with herself. The room was just too quiet without her.

"How do you feel about having dinner with my parents?"

Jeremiah looked sheepish, as if there was no way Brett could be expected to bear such a burden.

"Are you kidding?" she practically squealed, sitting up. "I love your family." Maybe she'd wear the new dual-strand freshwater pearl rope necklace she'd found at Pimpernel's—though it was usually a little too chichi for Brett's more eccentric taste, she'd had a desperate shopping craving last week and had dragged Jenny to the boutique. They'd tried on overpriced dresses they weren't planning on buying and ignored the scowls from the blond saleswoman who clearly did not appreciate the business of Waverly Owls—except the ones like Callie, who had charge accounts there. Pearls were not normally Brett's thing, a little too debutante for her, but these were funky and oddly shaped, and she could imagine someone like Sienna Miller tossing them around her neck to liven up any boring old black dress. They were actually just right for dinner with the Mortimers, who themselves were über-classy, with a little off-kilter friskiness to them.

"You don't mind?" Jeremiah shifted on the mat, causing Brett to slide closer to him. She certainly didn't mind *that*. "We can get a good dinner out of them, at least."

Brett placed her small, gold-ringed hand on Jeremiah's and leaned over him. "And then we can go out . . . and, uh, have a good time."

Jeremiah kissed her cheek and let his mouth linger there, so that she could feel the words as he spoke them. "I like the sound of that."

He was so adorable. She wanted to jump his bones. *Oh God. Not now*, Brett reminded herself. Her whole body tensed with anticipation. St. Lucius would certainly win their homecoming game, and Brett would stand on the sidelines cheering Jeremiah on, wearing some outfit that would make the St. Lucius girls weep with jealousy. After Jeremiah threw the winning touchdown and the fans rushed the field, she would run across the grass (note: don't wear spiky heels) and throw her arms around Jeremiah's padded shoulders, and he would spin her around and give her one of those dramatic, movie-ending kisses. They'd go out to dinner with his family, to St. Lucius's equivalent of Le Petit Coq, and Brett would dazzle the Mortimers with her knowledge of world affairs (note: browse through some *Newsweek*s at the library), all the while trying not to get too caught up in the sexy, devastating stares Jeremiah would shoot at her from across the table. After cheek-kissing Mr. and Mrs. Mortimer au revoir, she and Jeremiah would go somewhere very private, romantic, and perfect for them to lose their virginity together.

She snuggled her head into Jeremiah's shoulder, and as he squeezed her back, she thanked fate and her good sense for not letting her sleep with Mr. Dalton. Jeremiah was the one she had been saving herself for. And she only had to wait a few more days.

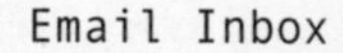

From: HeathFerro@waverly.edu
To: beerdude101@hotmail.com
Date: Wednesday, October 2, 6:49 p.m.
Subject: Delivery of da goods

Bro,

Thanks for the hook-up—six half-kegs should get the party started right. Remember where you dropped off last time? Go a little farther—the sixth building on the access road is Dumbarton, the lovely ladies' dorm. I'll meet you at the back.

Midnight. Whoohoo!!

H

OwlNet Instant Message Inbox

HeathFerro: Hey, frosh, remember that favor you owe me? I'm collecting.

JulianMcCafferty: Uh, what favor?

HeathFerro: Not kicking your ass for being a punk-ass freshman!

JulianMcCafferty: Freakin' hilarious. What do you want?

HeathFerro: It involves picking up a couple of kegs from behind Dumbarton. Maybe we'll get lucky and they'll be having a moonlight panty party.

JulianMcCafferty: When you put it that way . . .

HeathFerro: Knew you couldn't resist. Meet me downstairs at 12, unless it's past your bedtime?

JulianMcCafferty: I'll bring my blankie.

A WAVERLY OWL IS ALWAYS WILLING TO LEND A HAND TO A FELLOW OWL IN NEED.

Tinsley Carmichael slid open the first-floor window to her room, cringing when it creaked noisily before realizing she didn't give a fuck if it was almost midnight and Brett woke up. She glanced over at her roommate's inert body, buried beneath her funky hot-pink-and-fuchsia Indian print comforter, and almost smiled at how she always slept like she was in a coma. They'd learned to sleep through Callie's snoring and talking fits.

Tinsley sighed and eased herself up onto the windowsill, letting one silk-pajamaed leg hang out. She leaned back against the frame and shook a cigarette from her brand-new box of Marlboro Ultra Lights. After another long, tension-filled evening, smoking felt glorious. She was probably one of the only Dumbarton girls awake right now. On her way back from brushing her teeth, she ran into the meek little girl next door—wearing an ugly dark brown terry-cloth bathrobe and carrying a thick black towel over her shoulder. Um, okay. It was like the twelfth time Tinsley had seen her heading into the shower at an insanely late hour—apparently she could only shower when everyone else in the dorm was asleep. Sure, *that* was normal. And since Pardee never said anything about this girl clearly breaking lights-out curfew, she must either have something over on Pardee (maybe Tinsley wasn't the only one who'd caught her messing around with a married dean?) or Pardee let her break the rule because it was the only thing that kept her out of the loony bin.

Brett and Tinsley's roommate relationship rivaled only Callie and Jenny's in its fucked-up-ness. Brett was on Tinsley's shit list this year after two major friendship-ending offenses. First, she got all lovey-dovey with Jenny Humphrey, as if *Jenny* had been the one to save Brett's ass last year by taking the blame for the caught-in-the-playing-fields-with-Ecstasy incident. And then the whole Mr. Dalton thing—Brett was practically *sleeping* with the guy and couldn't be bothered to tell her. Tinsley couldn't help trying to steal Mr. Dalton. Lack of loyalty in best friends drove her insane.

Which is maybe why she was feeling a teeny bit bad—not *guilty*, just bad—about the way the Mr. Dalton saga played out. All she'd wanted was for Brett to welcome her back to Waverly with open arms—was that too much to ask for from one of her supposed best friends? She'd been hurt by Brett's coldness, and so she'd lashed out—a little harshly, yes. But Brett didn't have to take everything so *seriously*. It's not like she was going to *marry* Dalton or anything. Besides, as a direct result of Tinsley stealing Dalton away, Brett was back with Jeremiah. So really, things had all worked out. Brett should be down on her knees thanking her!

Tinsley sort of enjoyed the fight, especially now that Brett was fighting her back head-on. At first, Brett had avoided the room for a few days, but then it was like she realized she was missing out or something, so she started hanging around more, playing her music loudly, gabbing with Jeremiah or her sister on her cell phone, daring Tinsley to say something. Brett had even brought her geeky chemistry study group over one night to do flash cards of chemical equations and symbols—and Tinsley had simply sat silently at her desk, ignoring them as they called out things like Faraday's law of electrolysis and glucose reaction. Geeks! Just tonight, she and Brett had sat at their desks, five feet away from each other, writing papers on their laptops and listening to their iPods. Brett ended up going to bed first—in silence, of course.

Tinsley inhaled deeply. It was all a game. And Brett was bound to be the one to cave first.

Outside her window, something moved. Tinsley flicked her ash into the bushes beneath her and squinted—she was practically blind without her contacts. It looked like there were two figures out by the access road that ran behind Dumbarton and the other girls' dorms, next to what looked like a squadron of shiny UFOs. Was that . . . Heath??

Tinsley's heart started to beat a little faster. Something was up. She glanced behind her at the nearly comatose Brett, then lifted the Tiffany's key ring where her platinum Zippo and the emergency whistle (that her father made her promise to have with her at all times—even though she was at Waverly now, not South Africa) hung. She pressed it to her lips and gave a quick tweet.

The figures jumped, but before they could flee, Tinsley waved a pale, thin arm at them and flashed a peace sign. "That you, H.F.?" Tinsley whispered loudly into the cool dark night as Heath galloped toward her. She squinted harder at the figure next to him. It looked like that hot, super-tall freshman that was always hanging around the older boys. Julian? Excellent. Her night was definitely shaping up.

"Oh, baby!" Heath cried out in something slightly louder than a whisper. "Glad to see you!"

"What are you guys doing out here?" Tinsley demanded, dropping her eyes coyly. She felt very sexy, sitting in her window in her white silk Hanro pajamas, smoking a cigarette, like something out of a Tennessee Williams play. "It's, um, a little after curfew."

"We like to live dangerously," Julian replied, yawning. Tinsley turned her head to look at him. He was just as cute as she remembered, even with her blurred vision.

"Oh, yeah? Looking for 'shrooms again?" Tinsley kicked her hanging leg against the brick wall of Dumbarton and flicked her cigarette into the grass below.

Heath stepped on it with his sneaker and smashed it into the ground. "Look, we have a situation here." There was a worried look on Heath's normally laid-back face. He pointed at the UFOs. "We have six half-kegs that need a home."

Tinsley stared at the glistening silver lumps. Six half-kegs? "Why did you bring them *here*?"

Julian grinned and ran a hand through his shaggy blond hair. "As a present to you? An offering?"

"Can you hold the bullshit for a second, sweetheart?" Heath looked like he was wired on caffeine pills or something. "How about we work on problem-solving and save the flirting for later?"

"Why don't you just put them up on the roof?" Tinsley suggested innocently, shrugging and indicating the fire escape at the corner of the building that led all the way to the roof. This would be quite entertaining to watch. "No one will find them there."

"Brilliant!" Heath slapped his forehead. "I knew you'd think of something." He pushed Julian toward the kegs. "Grab one. We'll take it up the fire escape."

Boys are so dumb. Incredulously, and with a little too much pleasure, Tinsley watched as the two of them awkwardly lugged one of the half-keg barrels up the rickety wrought-iron fire escape, trying desperately not to make noise. She snickered. Were they high or just morons?

By the time they got back to the ground, Tinsley had had a change of heart. "Listen, I just heard the freaky girl next door head into the shower." Maybe the quiet girl who only showered when no one else around had a use after all. She'd be honored. "Why don't I just let you in the back door—you can sneak them into her room. She's got a single. I bet they'll fit under her bed."

She took her time sliding into her cushy Ugg slippers (she hated the boots, but the slippers were okay) and padding down the hall and down the cold marble steps to the back door of Dumbarton. Heath and Julian were waiting for her, gasping from having lugged the half kegs into position.

"You guys are in bad shape," Tinsley whispered, pressing herself against the door so that the boys could pass by, each carrying one of the heavy containers in his arms.

"Why don't you help us, then?" Heath whispered back crankily, his sneakers, wet with dew, squeaking against the floorboards.

"I think I've done *more* than enough already." She led them down the hall, noting, as they passed the bathroom, that the shower was still running.

"Who takes a shower at midnight?" Heath glanced around at all the closed dorm room doors they passed as if imagining the sleeping, naked girls inside. He'd forgotten all about being cranky and looked perfectly blissful.

"No one you want to know." Light peeked out from beneath Shower Girl's closed door and Tinsley threw it open. It was a small room that must have once been a storage closet, as neat and tidy as a monk's cell. The bed was propped up on giant cinder blocks, raising it a good foot off the hardwood floor.

"Hot," Heath whispered, running his hands across the smooth bedspread, which sported an enormous Superman logo. Or maybe it was Batman. Tinsley hated all that superhero shit, but Heath looked like he was about to throw himself down on it and start humping.

Tinsley slapped his hand off the bed. "Stop drooling over

Catwoman and start acting useful. Don't you have some kegs to hide?" She lifted the edge of the blanket and leaned over to peek under the bed. Completely empty. Wow, this girl didn't even have any shit. "It's empty under here—they'll fit."

"Catwoman?" Heath scoffed as he gently set his half keg on the ground and pushed it under the bed. "She's got a bat on her boobs—it's Batgirl!"

"You mean like Alicia Silverstone?" Julian straightened up after shoving his keg in place.

Heath groaned. "No! That was a cruel bastardization of the real Batgirl, who has a genius-level intellect, superb computer-hacking skills, and more martial arts . . ."

Julian and Tinsley exchanged glances. Tinsley grabbed Heath by the hand and pulled him toward the door. "You know how I love to hear you wax all poetic about cartoons and everything, but that girl is probably all shampooed and conditioned, so can we focus here?"

"Right." Heath headed for the door, giving one last lingering look over his shoulder. Julian looked amused. In fact, Tinsley noticed he always had that expression on his face, as if life in general entertained him. As they tiptoed back down the hall and out the back door, a beam of moonlight hit his cheek and Tinsley forgot all about being jealous that Heath Ferro was dreaming of hooking up with the loser girl next door just so he could roll around on her geeky bedspread.

All she could think about was putting the first serious expression in Julian's eyes. Even if he was just a freshman, she was going to make him fall in love with her.

OwlNet Email Inbox

From: JLWalsh@lockwoodwalshbarristers.com
To: EasyWalsh@waverly.edu
Date: Thursday, October 3, 8:12 a.m.
Subject: Dinner

E,

Tried calling but no response. In town for Trustees Weekend. Will meet you for dinner on Friday night at Le Petit Coq. 8 sharp. I'm making a reservation for three. Bring Callie.

J.L.W.

A WAVERLY OWL NEVER FORGETS WHO HIS GIRLFRIEND IS.

Thursday morning, Easy Walsh strode across the quad, barely glancing down at the puddles left over from yesterday's rain that his brown-and-tan Golas narrowly avoided. His eyes were glued to his Moleskine notebook, the one he used to jot down notes from Mr. Wilde's lectures. Problem was, he was often more interested in sketching what he saw outside the window—an overfed squirrel trying to stick its nose into a crumpled pack of cigarettes, two girls in tank tops playing Frisbee, Heath Ferro reading *People* magazine—than paying attention to what his teacher had to say about manifest destiny and the Articles of Confederation. Easy flipped through the pages of sketches and his own barely decipherable writing and sighed. Twenty minutes of cramming was not going to help him pass this test.

Even though he'd known about the test for two weeks, Easy

hadn't been able to bring himself to study. There were just too many other more important things. How could he be expected to hit the books when the leaves were changing color and Credo could smell the brisk scent of autumn and practically begged him to take her out riding? When winter came, it would be too cold to paint out in his secret spot in the woods. He had to take advantage of it now. He didn't understand people who spent their whole lives doing things they *thought* they should do—they were never happy, were they?

He closed the notebook and lit a Marlboro Red.

The email from his dad this morning had irritated him more than he wanted to admit. He hadn't yet told his dad about breaking up with Callie. Not that he ever confided in his dad. Easy and his father were exact opposites. Jefferson Linford Walsh, graduate of Waverly, Vanderbilt, and Yale Law School, partner in a high-profile southern law firm, father of four boys, three of them so far following almost perfectly in his footsteps, while the youngest one was an artsy fuckup who could barely manage to study for his first major AP History exam.

Easy grabbed his phone and punched in his father's private extension.

"J. L. Walsh speaking," his father's voice boomed, his Kentucky accent more pronounced than Easy's.

Easy exhaled a puff of smoke and watched it float up into the trees. "Dad. Hey."

"It sounds like you're smoking," his dad observed, forgoing more common greetings like, "How are you? Good morning! Good to hear your voice, son!"

Easy flicked his cigarette to the ground. "Nice to talk to you too."

Mr. Walsh sighed. "I hope you're not calling to try and extract yourself from our dinner appointment on Friday night."

Dinner appointment? Never have a lawyer for a father. "No, dinner is fine." Easy lay down on top of a nearby picnic table. The warm sun had baked it dry after yesterday's downpours, but the table still felt a little damp through his jeans and blazer. Still, it was much easier to talk to J. L. Walsh when lying down. "But I'm not going out with Callie anymore. And I'm sort of seeing . . ."

"Are you kidding me?" His father's voice raised a stern octave when he was upset. Easy felt his body tense up and his brain sent an apology to his lips before he could do anything to stop it. Luckily his father barked out orders over the top of it and Easy realized he was talking to his secretary.

"Well, then, she'll just have to be my guest instead," his father continued, his voice easing back to its natural pitch. Easy could hear him scratching on one of his famous yellow legal pads. "I like Callie. I'd like to see her."

"*Dad . . .*"

"I'll see you both there at eight sharp. Looking forward to it. Anything else?"

Was there anything else? Easy wasn't really interested in getting into a giant discussion about it, especially since the more Easy protested, the more his father insisted. Better to just let it go. His dad could complain about Callie's absence all he wanted over his coq au vin.

"See you then." Easy clicked his phone shut and slipped it back into the pocket of his baggy Levi's. He settled back onto the picnic table and closed his eyes, taking deep breaths of fresh autumn air and ruminating on how screwed he was.

"Does taking a nap before the test help you remember things?" A feminine voice broke into Easy's reverie. He propped himself up on his elbow and squinted. Callie was standing next to the table, wearing a white cardigan over a blue short-sleeved dress with a deep V neck that might have looked sleazy on some girls but looked fine on Callie, whose breasts, ever since she'd apparently stopped eating, had disappeared. She was teetering on one of her typical pairs of expensive-looking, pointy-toed heels, her new short haircut making her look younger and cuter than Easy was used to.

He blinked. Was she here to give him a hard time? Even though they were in the same history class, it was a big class, and Callie sat near the front with the rest of the girls who wanted an unimpeded view of Mr. Wilde, who'd been the studly teacher on campus before skeevy Mr. Dalton had arrived. Easy tended to sneak in late and escape the second class was over, especially now that he was avoiding Callie. Their breakup had gotten so ugly, even weeks later, he couldn't help wanting to avoid her—not for his sake so much as for hers. Waverly was a small place and it was notoriously hard to avoid people, but he wanted to do what he could to give Callie her space. Maybe she'd cool off and not hate him so much. Or maybe she'd stop hating Jenny, who was probably the most unhateable person ever. Callie was scary when she was pissed.

Once, when he'd forgotten their six-month anniversary, she had taken his copy of *On the Road* and torn out every fifth page. But now here she was, standing in front of him, *smiling*?

Easy sat up and swung his feet onto the bench below. "Nah, I think I'm pretty hopeless."

"Maybe if you wanted to impress Mr. Wilde as much as I did, you'd be ready for the test." She swung her expensive-looking honey-colored leather tote from one arm to the other.

"Hasn't everyone learned their lesson yet about obsessing over hot young teachers?" He rolled his eyes.

"Mr. Wilde is *married*. And has, like, two little girls," Callie pointed out. "Besides, he's *old*. He's, like, thirty-five or something."

Easy found himself laughing, something that felt good after his strained conversation with his dad. It was nice to see Callie in a good mood—one that did not include her nagging him about how she'd seen him flirting with someone else or giving him a hard time about playing Xbox with the guys instead of calling her and listening to her prattle on about her newest Barneys purchase. But now she seemed . . . more mellow. Maybe they could be friends after all? It really kind of sucked to be close to someone for so long and then suddenly not be *anything* anymore. It felt good to just be talking to her again. "Thirty-five is not old." Easy wiped his hand across his face. "Try forty-eight. That's when men are old. And cranky."

"Huh?" A confused look came across Callie's face. "Did you just talk to your dad or something?"

"Yeah. Charming as always." A rebellious curl fell in front

of Easy's eyes, and he swiped at it. "He'll be in town this weekend for the trustees' meetings. And he . . . uh . . . invited you to dinner with us on Friday," Easy found himself adding.

"He did?" She sounded surprised but pleased. "I can't believe he remembered my name!"

"Apparently you made quite an impression on him. Must be the southern girl thing." Callie could be totally charming when she wanted to be. When Easy's parents met her at Family Weekend last spring, they were completely smitten with her warm Georgia accent, confident demeanor, long strawberry blond hair, and ability to make sparkling conversation and come up with things to say even at awkward moments. He knew that she was used to having to make small talk at her governor mom's horribly stuffy political dinners and society events and that she kind of got a kick out of it. As his parents fawned all over her, they were probably picturing a big, fancy-pants wedding at the Governor's Mansion. Please.

"Do you . . ." Callie started to ask, then stopped and bit her cotton candy pink lower lip. "I mean, if it makes your life easier, I'm happy to come." Her hazel eyes, for once, seemed completely absent of an agenda. "If you want."

She was being really . . . nice. An image flashed through Easy's mind of what dinner with his father, alone, would be like—fielding relentless questions on every single class he was taking, asking about grades, wanting to know about his preparations for the SATs, his plans for college, his career, the Future. Then he pictured Callie there, charming the pants off stuffy old Dad, asking him about the law firm, telling funny anecdotes about her mother's political campaign, maybe even making J. L. Walsh laugh and act like a human being.

It wasn't much of a choice.

"Well, uh, if you don't mind . . . that would be . . . um . . . great."

Callie smiled. "Sweet. It'll be nice to see old J. L. again." She glanced at the silver-and-diamond wristwatch hung loosely around her slim wrist. She nodded toward Farnsworth Hall, looming behind them like a ghost. "We should get in there. He's going to pass out the test soon."

Easy groaned and stood up. The test. He grabbed his grubby army green canvas bag and slung it over his shoulder. "Great."

"And hey, don't worry, I won't tell Jenny." She slid both hands through her shoulder-length hair and Easy forced himself to look away from her elegant, pretty neck, suddenly overwhelmed with guilt.

Jenny. Shit. The whole time he'd been talking to Callie, Jenny hadn't once crossed his mind. Was that totally weird that he was bringing his ex-girlfriend to dinner with his dad instead of his current girlfriend? Yeah, that sounded pretty fucked up.

But then he tried to picture sweet little Jenny at the table with his dad, trying to answer all the questions he bombarded her with, one after another, lawyer style, until she burst into tears. Jenny didn't know what a hardass his father could be; she definitely needed to go through extensive preparations before being subjected to anything as demanding as a dinner date.

And Callie knew his dad already and knew how to handle his blustery demands. And it kind of felt like . . . they were friends now. There wasn't anything wrong with taking a friend out to eat with your dad, right?

But as he slid into his seat at the back of the room, he had a sinking feeling in the pit of his stomach, and he suspected it wasn't entirely due to the history exam he was about to flunk.

Email Inbox

From: TinsleyCarmichael@waverly.edu
To: CallieVernon@waverly.edu; BennyCunningham@waverly.edu; VerenaArneval@waverly.edu; CelineColista@waverly.edu; SageFrancis@waverly.edu; AlisonQuentin@waverly.edu
Date: Thursday, October 3, 5:55 p.m.
Subject: Put on your party shoes

Ladies,

Through a very fortuitous twist of fate, something special has just happened to fall into our laps or rather, on our roof . . . and we must take advantage of our good fortune!

Keg party, Dumbarton roof. 8 p.m. Shhh . . . Pardee has a couple of girlfriends over tonight—we saw them with several bottles of very cheap red wine, so you know what that means. I think it's safe to say that she'll be MIA.

Please tell Emily Jenkins her presence is requested—I think it's about time we added a new member to Café Society.

xxx,

Tinsley

WHEN NOT INVITED TO A PARTY, A WAVERLY OWL MAKES HER OWN FUN.

"Crazy Daizy or Maliblu?" Brett asked, holding up two brightly colored bottles of Pinkie Swear nail polish for Jenny to examine. The two of them were sprawled out on the floor of Dumbarton 303, leaning against the spare bed, the one formerly occupied by Tinsley Carmichael. Jenny's old cot had been returned to storage in the basement, and she had taken over Brett's bed—the thought of sleeping in the bed that Tinsley had been kicked out of creeped her out. All necessary equipment for at-home manicures was spread out between them: bowls of warm, soapy water to soften their nail beds, orangewood cuticle stick, nail file/buffer, creamy Bliss hand lotion, stacks of cotton pads, bottles of clear base-coat polish, Q-Tips, nail polish remover. It was like Rescue Salon or, at least, as close as you could get to it at Waverly.

Brett had suggested a mani-pedi night earlier that day, and Jenny was thrilled. Apparently it was something Callie and Tinsley and Brett had done all the time, and Jenny was pleased that Brett felt comfortable enough with her now to sort of let her fill their intimidating shoes. Jenny imagined that their mani-pedi nights had never been as mellow as this, though. From what Jenny had seen of their interactions, they were always fraught with underlying intensity and competitiveness. It seemed like each of them was desperate to come off as much cooler, more sophisticated than the others. Even Brett could get completely wrapped up in one-upping Tinsley and Callie.

"Um, Maliblu's a little too funky for me." Jenny wrinkled her nose at the sparkly blue bottle. "I don't think I can get away with blue nails." Her toes, stuffed uncomfortably into one of those foamy toe-separator cushions, were painted a bright cherry red. Vanessa Abrams, her brother Dan's high school girlfriend who was now living in Jenny's old room in her dad's West End Ave apartment, was the kind of girl who could pull off dark blue nail polish. With her shaved head and black-centric wardrobe, it would look almost natural. Not that she'd ever bother with a pedicure.

"I thought artists were supposed to be daring," Brett teased, and pressed the little bottle into Jenny's palm, careful not to smudge her still-wet base coat.

Jenny picked up the polish and examined it. She could be pretty boring sometimes. Why not give something new a try? "Do you think it glows in the dark?"

"I guess you'll have to get Easy alone to test it out." Brett had put the blue color on her toes already, and she wiggled them happily.

"We're supposed to go out to dinner tomorrow night," Jenny confessed, pressing the tiny brush against her thumbnail and watching the polish spread. It was less Manic Panic, more blackberry glaze, and not bad at all. "It'll be nice—I feel like I haven't gotten to see much of him lately."

"And how much of Easy do you want to see?" Brett asked suggestively, and shook a lock of her wild red hair out of her face, trying not to use her hands.

At the exact same moment, the door opened and Callie entered, wearing a stunning light blue Michael Kors dress and camel Jimmy Choo leather slingbacks that probably hadn't even appeared in the pages of *Vogue* yet. Jenny and Brett exchanged glances, but Callie was clearly set on pretending like she hadn't just heard her ex-boyfriend's name mentioned. In fact, to Jenny's absolute shock, Callie even sort of looked at her. It wasn't a smile, exactly, but it wasn't the same you-don't-even-exist-to-me look that Callie had been shooting her for the last few weeks, ever since she'd found out about her and Easy. Maybe she was thawing?

"Hey, Cal," Brett offered, watching as Callie stepped around the two girls on the floor and headed over to her closet. "I like your dress—and shoes. Are they new?"

Callie threw open her closet door and stood there, deep in thought, as if she hadn't heard Brett. "What?" she said a moment later as, in one motion, she pulled the dress over her head and tossed it carelessly over the rack in Tinsley's old closet, which she had taken over the second Tinsley's things moved downstairs. "Oh, uh, yeah. New."

Brett and Jenny exchanged a look. Jenny's brown eyes widened and she mouthed the words "*Everything's* new" to Brett. Brett nodded, looking concerned. Apparently Callie was notorious for overspending whenever she was feeling depressed. Last year, when she'd failed a chemistry final, she'd maxed out her Visa Platinum card at Saks.com, even though it had an unfathomable limit. Jenny could see Brett's eyes running over the stacks of shoe boxes. Enough to build a village out of cardboard. If Jenny's anarchist-communist father had seen them, he would have shaken his head and muttered something cutting about conspicuous consumption. Secretly, Jenny thought it was kind of exotic to treat depression in such an extravagant way.

Jenny leaned against the bed and watched as Callie stood in front of her closet, her bony shoulder blades sticking out even more than usual. Obviously she didn't have to worry about bingeing when she was down. She pulled a flimsy mauve dress, whose Jill Stuart tags still hung off the zipper, from the closet. "Can you zip me, B.?" she said absently, glancing over her bare shoulder, her strawberry blond hair swishing against her neck. She tossed a faint smile in Jenny's direction as Brett zipped her up.

"Hold on—you've still got your tags." Brett bent over and grabbed the nail clippers from where they were lying near Jenny's toes. "Pretty dress. Where're you going?" Tiny strands of silver thread glittered in the light as Callie spun in a circle.

"Oh." She examined herself in the full-length mirror next to her overcrowded closet. She wrinkled her nose guiltily, but clearly she didn't *feel* guilty. "Sorry. Secret Society only."

Right, Brett thought, her feelings of tenderness for Callie immediately evaporating. If she was going to keep on being Tinsley's stooge, she could go ahead and zip up her own fucking designer dresses.

Brett sat back down on the floor across from Jenny, trying not to show her irritation. She yawned. "Have fun." She made her voice sound as uninterested as possible, as if they were talking about a Latin class and not a party.

Wait a second . . . Was that the sound of people walking around on the *roof?*

"I would ask you to come," Callie said, pulling a pair of dangling white gold earrings from her satin jewelry box, her voice dripping with fake sweetness that even the most tone-deaf social outcast could see through. "But . . ." She trailed off.

"That's totally sweet of you." Brett opened the bottle of Crazy Daizy and took a deep breath. She wasn't going to let Callie piss her off *and* mess up her nails. Jenny was busy pretending to be completely engrossed in applying a clear top coat to her toes, but Brett could tell she was trying hard not to laugh. "We're actually a little busy here."

Callie didn't look up as she carefully applied her Dior eyeliner in Precious Violet. "Right. Manicures. Go crazy." She blinked slowly in the mirror, then loudly slapped the cap back on her eyeliner wand.

Brett's green eyes narrowed, but she kept a playful lilt in

her voice as a blob of peach polish dropped off the brush and landed on her bare knee. "Granted, it's not giving Heath Ferro a lap dance or anything über-classy like that," she observed tersely, getting a jab in about the last society party. "But at least I'll have nice nails in the morning!"

"Yeah, well. Have an awesome time." When Callie opened the door to the room, dance music flooded in. "Later!" Her voice trilled insincerely as she slammed the door behind her.

"That went well." Jenny giggled. "I mean, at least she *looked* at me."

Brett felt a little nervous. "I don't know. I just hope she's not trying to be someone she's not, you know?" Callie seemed more Tinsley-like just now than Tinsley herself, and the idea of two Tinsleys walking around campus was truly terrifying.

Instant Message Inbox

YvonneStidder: What's on the roof? I got a big concert. Can't hear my sax.

KaraWhalen: It's Tinsley, etc. A kegger or something.

YvonneStidder: A keg on the roof? Cool! I'm there!

KaraWhalen: Good luck with that. Bitches only.

YvonneStidder: Hey, we live here too.

KaraWhalen: Do we?

Instant Message Inbox

SageFrancis: Get to the roof, stat, you lucky bitch.

EmilyJenkins: About fucking time! What should I wear?? My Marc Jacobs?

SageFrancis: Whatever. Just remember to kiss Tinsley's ass.

EmilyJenkins: Boys too?

SageFrancis: Um, no. And no Parker DuBois, either. Anyway, he's just not that into you.

EmilyJenkins: Whatev. I'm IN!!!!!!!!!!!

A WAVERLY OWL DOES NOT ALIGHT UPON THE ROOF OF ANY SCHOOL BUILDING.

Thursday night was warm, and as soon as the sun dipped below the horizon, the party on the roof started to heat up. Tinsley had kept an eye on the keg on the roof all day, checking to make sure it was securely hidden in the shade and replacing the ice in the cooler when it melted down. Standing on the roof now in her gold metallic leather Giuseppe Zanotti boots and Gold Hawk cream-colored silk skirt with hand-crocheted trim, paired with a simple white tee, the light wind billowing the skirt against her thighs, she felt—peaceful. Which, when translated, meant—bored. The taboo roof of Dumbarton was surprisingly dull: the brick walls shielded the girls from a view of anything other than the tops of some trees. The brightly colored leaves looked quite majestic as they faded into the dusk. Majestic and boring.

Tinsley leaned back in her plastic lawn chair, one of the half dozen that Sage and Celine had snatched from the storage room in the basement, and sipped her cold beer. All the Café Society girls were there, and she had almost forgotten that little Jenny Humphrey and bitchy Brett had once been part of this group. *Almost*. It irritated Tinsley that Brett Messerschmidt seemed so unaffected by her social dismissal. She'd expected her former friend to be ostracized by everyone at Waverly once it became known she was on the permanent outs with Tinsley Carmichael. But things hadn't happened like that. Brett seemed to be doing fine, still hanging out with the other girls when Tinsley wasn't around as if she hadn't been blacklisted. Tinsley was still waiting for Brett to throw herself down to the floor, kiss the toes of her boots, and beg her to let them start all over. But Brett seemed so . . . over it.

Maybe it was because Brett was back in love with Jeremiah. Of course the star quarterback's girlfriend would always be popular—as long as they were together, that is.

The metal door to the roof banged open, interrupting Tinsley's thoughts. It was Callie, wearing one of her gorgeous new dresses. "The natives are getting restless down there," she said pointedly to Tinsley as she stepped gingerly over a cinder block. "They all want to crash our party. Well, not Jenny and Brett," Callie corrected herself bitterly, her lips screwed up into a pretty pink pout. "They're in my room giving each other gay manicures or something."

Tinsley adjusted her tiered cream-colored skirt around and inhaled deeply. She surveyed the scene—Alison Quentin and

Verena Arneval were dancing to the music coming from Tinsley's iPod. Benny Cunningham and Celine Colista were huddled around the keg, trying to design a new drinking game—one that hadn't been played ten thousand times before. Sage Francis was chatting with Emily Jenkins, their newest member, something Tinsley began to regret the second Emily appeared on the roof wearing what looked like a Macy's prom dress from 1991.

Tinsley sighed heavily. She didn't want to admit it out loud, but this party was . . . lame. She was bored. Bored. Bored. Bored. "Well, hell." She stood up. "Let's invite 'em in."

Callie's pink mouth opened in surprise. "Are you serious?"

"Why the hell not?" Tinsley strode carelessly toward the door, downing her beer on the way.

"Because it's like . . . Yvonne the British band geek, and that stringy-haired girl who has, like, a picture of Jewel on her door, and these . . ."

Tinsley paused and patted her hand against Callie's cheek. "Don't be such a snob, honey." Her violet eyes sparkled with amusement. This could be interesting. "There's plenty of beer for everyone."

"Whatever." Callie rolled her eyes.

Feeling unpredictable and magnanimous, an SAT word she never thought she'd use to describe herself, Tinsley pulled open the creaky metal door. Several girls scurried out of the way, but a few others hung back, eternally optimistic. Well, why not give them a thrill?

"Hey, girls." Tinsley's eyes expertly scanned the vaguely

familiar faces—girls she had seen in classes or the cafeteria or maybe even in the bathroom, brushing their teeth at the next sink. Girls she didn't really know and girls she wasn't terribly interested in knowing. She recognized Yvonne, the nerdy band girl in her Italian class, who, with her tiny bird-like body and long blond hair, might be pretty if she didn't wear such dweeby clothes.

Magnanimous. Tinsley forced a smile to her red glossy lips. "Why don't you come up to the party? It's such a nice night."

"Really?" Yvonne piped up. "You don't mind?"

Christ, Tinsley thought. Did she have to beg? "Sure," Tinsley said through gritted teeth. "Come on up. Invite all the others—it'll be an all-dorm bonding thing." Immediately she remembered that Callie said Brett and Jenny were having a mani-pedi party, one of the things the three of *them* used to do in better days. Days when they actually spoke to each other. She'd be damned if those traitors were going to come to this party, all-dorm or not. "I'll go tell the third floor."

Yvonne and a couple of her dopey friends ran downstairs, eager to spread the good news to the other Dumbarton dorks. Tinsley smiled to herself as she strutted down the third-floor hallway, deliberately ignoring room 303. She couldn't resist pausing for a second in front of it, however, just to see if they were talking about her. The room was quiet except for the low hum of a hair dryer. How disappointing.

An hour later, approximately twenty-five girls were crowded on the roof and sprawled out in lawn chairs, chatting excitedly. The more the girls drank, the quieter the music seemed—so the volume on the iPod sound deck had crept steadily higher. But everyone was too happy emptying the keg and dancing around the central air-conditioning unit to notice. The stars had come out, and Tinsley lay on her back on one of the padded lounge chairs next to Callie.

"You have to admit, this was a great idea." Tinsley's voice was dreamy, and she couldn't help thinking that maybe the party would have been even better if some boys had been there. Namely, a tall, sexy freshman with bleached-out dirty-blond hair that hung to his chin. A perverse smile came to Tinsley's lips just thinking about Julian.

Callie opened her mouth to reply sarcastically, but whatever she was about to say was cut off by a sudden shout from below, somewhere near the front door of Dumbarton.

"Freeze! Who's up there?"

The girls stopped dancing, immobilized by fear.

"Don't move! We're coming up!"

Immediately, as if a fire had broken out or someone had announced a clearance sale at Neiman Marcus, the girls pulled open the roof door and flew down the stairs, desperate to return to their rooms before Marymount or Mrs. Pardee or whoever the hell it was out there managed to reach them. Looking almost gleeful, Tinsley scooped up her iPod sound deck and joined the mad rush down the back stairs, only remembering the nearly empty, abandoned keg when it was too late to retrieve it.

Instant Message Inbox

EmilyJenkins: Was that really Marymount? Are we screwed?

CelineColista: Totally.

EmilyJenkins: My first society party and Tinsley let all the losers come up? Hello?

CelineColista: Um . . . three hours ago you were one of those losers!

EmilyJenkins: Don't remind me.

Instant Message Inbox

YvonneStidder: Just wanted to give you a heads-up—Marymount and Pardee are knocking on all the first-floor doors. Asked why you and Brett aren't in your room—I said you were upstairs in Callie's. K?

TinsleyCarmichael: Are they asking about the party?

YvonneStidder: Not really. Pardee looks trashed. I think Marymount crashed her girls-night party.

TinsleyCarmichael: Interesting . . .

Email Inbox

To: Dumbarton Residents
From: DeanMarymount@waverly.edu
Date: Thursday, October 3, 10:16 p.m.
Subject: Disciplinary Committee

Residents of Dumbarton dormitory,

I am extremely disappointed to announce that tonight, after a teacher reported a noise disturbance in Dumbarton Hall, I discovered a keg of beer on the roof of the dormitory.

All residents of Dumbarton are to appear before the Disciplinary Committee. The meeting will take place in board room 3 on the first floor of Stansfield Hall tomorrow morning, at 10 a.m.

Attendance obligatory.

Dean Marymount

A WAVERLY OWL ACCEPTS HER PUNISHMENT WITH GRACE AND APLOMB.

Brett was irritated about the last-minute Disciplinary Committee meeting, even though she did appreciate getting pulled out of her mind-numbingly dull chemistry class with Mr. Frye. At quarter to ten, just when the other students were strapping on their sweat-inducing plastic goggles and chemical-proof aprons, Brett, Benny, and Celine all gathered their things, and Professor Frye gave them an absentminded nod, his hands already full of clattering glass test tubes.

"This bites," Celine grumbled the second the lab door closed behind them. "But at least we missed out on the goggles." Celine's black hair slid in front of her eyes and she touched her fingertips to her smooth olive skin. "Those things leave indentations on your forehead for, like, an hour."

"Today was my turn with Lon Baruzza as a lab partner," whined Benny. "You know I've been waiting for that forever."

She gripped her stick-straight light brown hair in her fists and tugged in anguish.

"He does have a really nice ass." Celine pushed open the front door of the science center and the three girls headed down the steps and toward Stansfield Hall. "But you could get close to that without having to be his lab partner," she pointed out with a giggle.

Brett rolled her eyes, her mind on other things. It had sounded like the whole freaking dorm was on the roof last night. Not that Brett *wanted* to be there or anything, but it still would have been nice if someone had asked.

Whatever. At least now she wasn't the one in trouble. As Benny and Celine prattled on, Brett kept her face composed, knowing she looked completely innocent in her pale pink Nanette Lepore baby doll dress, black leggings, and pale gray Sigerson Morrison ballet flats. She smiled to herself. Even her nails looked nice.

Once inside the Stansfield board room, Brett headed over to the committee side of the enormous table with Benny and Celine right behind her. Rows of girls in uncomfortable-looking folding chairs stared out at her from across the room, their knees pressed together primly, maroon blazers neatly buttoned. It was weird to see so many defendants for a DC case—usually it was one or two stray delinquents, although once the whole Thespian Society had been summoned after they famously performed *Our Town* wearing only Saran wrap.

Dean Marymount, wearing a tie with Van Gogh sunflowers splattered all over it, entered the room and immediately stopped short at the sight of Brett and the other DC girls sitting on their accustomed side of the table. "Ladies." He made a shooing gesture with his hands. "Please take a seat with the rest of your dormmates." He gave them a withering look as if they should have known better.

Brett's jaw dropped, and she glanced at Benny, who looked equally surprised. "Sir?" Brett spoke up. "But we . . . I—"

Marymount cut her off. "You three live in Dumbarton, don't you?" Marymount didn't wait for an answer and sat down at the end of the table, shuffling through the papers in his hands.

Well, then. Her cheeks flushed as red as her hair, Brett stood up in a huff and headed over to where Jenny was sitting in the front row. She flopped into the empty seat next to her. "We didn't even go to their stupid party," she growled under her breath.

Jenny patted Brett's arm. "It'll be okay. What can they do? Suspend us for doing our nails in our dorm room?"

"You'll see," Brett replied skeptically.

Jenny's chocolate-colored eyes looked vaguely worried as the two of them watched the room fill up with girls. It was totally weird for Brett to be on *this* side of the table. The girls were biting their manicured nails and tapping the toes of their shoes against the shiny wooden floor, whispering to each other a little too loudly.

"Asshole," Jenny heard someone say. At the table, Ryan Reynolds and the non-Dumbarton members of the DC, mostly freshmen and sophomores, had taken their seats next to petite Miss Rose of the English Department, who had taken over as the temporary DC adviser after Mr. Dalton's resignation. With her black turtleneck beneath her probably size-zero maroon blazer and her dark brown hair pulled back into a neat ponytail, she could have easily passed for a freshman.

"Let's get started, shall we?" Marymount looked tired, his round wire-rimmed glasses making his small blue eyes seem even smaller. He continued to flip through the papers in his hand, which Brett guessed had absolutely nothing at all to do with the keg bust last night. He just liked his props. "Mr. Wilde, you were the first one to notice the, um, *gathering* while walking by Dumbarton last night, correct?"

"Yes, correct." Mild-mannered Mr. Wilde looked uncomfortable in his role as disciplinarian. He was one of those teachers who really cared whether or not his AP History students liked him, and the walls of his office were plastered with posters of album covers—not just ones from his generation, but ones the kids would respect too—OutKast, Coldplay, Interpol. He looked like it killed him to be here, getting his students in trouble. He tugged obsessively at his collar. "I was on my way home from the library when I heard some . . . uh . . . loud music. There appeared to be people dancing on the roof of the dorm."

Marymount tapped his silver pen against the mahogany table. "What did you do next?" he prompted.

"I called security," Mr. Wilde admitted apologetically. "Then I shouted up to the girls to stay where they were. By the time I knocked on Mrs. Pardee's door"—he paused and blushed, and there was some twittering in the crowd of girls since everyone knew that Pardee had had some girlfriends over last night for a wine-drinking pajama party—"and the two of us got up to the roof, they'd all disappeared into their rooms."

Marymount cleared his throat. "And so it's not really clear how many were there—or who had been there, correct?"

"Correct," Mr. Wilde confirmed. "But they'd left an almost-empty keg behind—and a trash bag full of plastic cups." He took a sip from his cup of coffee.

"Were there a lot of cups?"

Brett kicked Jenny's foot. Who cared?

"The trash bag was almost full."

"Thank you." Marymount flitted his eyes over the group of girls for the first time since they'd started. "Girls, I know you are all aware that the consumption of alcoholic beverages is behavior we cannot tolerate." Brett could tell he was attempting to look sternly in each of the girls' eyes, but he gave up halfway through and began to glare at the table. "The timing of this incident is especially unfortunate, as we are preparing to host the trustees on campus this weekend and do not have time to babysit you." Marymount sighed, something Brett noticed that he did often during DC meetings to give the impression that he was terribly unhappy about being their headmaster in the first place. "Unfortunately, because it is not apparent who exactly the guilty parties are, we are going to have to punish you all."

"No fucking way," Brett gasped.

A murmur ran through the crowd, which Marymount immediately silenced by shouting over it. "Beginning tomorrow evening after dinner, you will all be under house arrest for the weekend and confined to Dumbarton Hall until Monday morning. Meals will be brought in, and any girl seen leaving the residency will face serious consequences."

Serious consequences? What about not being able to go to Jeremiah's homecoming game? Or out to dinner with his parents or out to the St. Lucius parties to show all those St. Lucius girls that Jeremiah was off the market? Or to lose her virginity! "This is so unfair!" Brett exclaimed loudly, though her voice was drowned out by the exclamations and complaints of the two dozen other girls.

Marymount cleared his throat and rapped his knuckles on the table. There was more? "I know there may be some of you who were not involved in the keg party, and I'm sure you think this is an unfair punishment." A murmur of agreement went up and Marymount quickly continued. "*However*, to be aware of rule-breaking and to do nothing about it is, in the administration's eyes, comparable to rule-breaking itself." He looked directly at Brett as he said this, and her face flushed with anger. Not ratting on your dormmates for having a kegger was as bad as actually sneaking a keg into a dormitory and getting plastered? He had to be kidding!

For the first time, Miss Rose spoke up, her small voice surprisingly authoritative. "The committee has decided that in addition to the house arrest, the girls of Dumbarton must each hand in on Monday morning a written report on what you've learned about being a responsible Owl." Ryan Reynolds, who'd been gazing affectionately at Miss Rose the whole time Marymount was talking, was now busy trying to hold back the smirk on his face, clearly amused by the whole thing. He met Brett's gaze over the fat bowl of white carnations sitting in the middle of the table and gave her a wink. He was always skeezing on her during meetings, and he was probably all turned on by the fact that the class prefect was suddenly one of the delinquents.

But Brett was too busy being pissed off to be grossed out by Ryan. This was insane. Not only was her weekend ruined, but now she had to sit down and write some crap about what it means to be a responsible Owl? Fuck that.

"I don't want anything like this to happen again." Marymount stood up, looking more disgusted than Brett had ever seen him. It was like he couldn't bear to look at them anymore, and suddenly Brett felt ashamed. Dean Marymount was a dork, of course, but she wanted him to think highly of her. Now it seemed like he thought she was just like everyone else, and she hadn't even done anything! "You are dismissed and may return to your classes."

A responsible Owl? Brett thought bitterly. *A responsible Owl shits all over Tinsley Carmichael.*

Instant Message Inbox

CallieVernon: Ugh. This sucks.

TinsleyCarmichael: Hey, don't get all depressed. HF brought over six mini-kegs . . . they only found the tapped one on the roof.

CallieVernon: No fucking way. Where are they stashed?

TinsleyCarmichael: Under depresso girl next door's bed . . . bet they'll come in handy this weekend.

CallieVernon: Aren't we in enough trouble?

TinsleyCarmichael: A responsible Owl does not let an opportunity like this go to waste!

A WORTHY OWL ALWAYS NOTICES HIS GIRLFRIEND'S NAILS, EVEN IF HIS THOUGHTS ARE ELSEWHERE.

Friday was a chilly, gray day, as if Marymount had ordered the weather to punish the girls of Dumbarton too. Like being confined to the dorm for the entire weekend wasn't punishment enough. Or unfair enough.

"Marymount bites," Alison Quentin muttered as she and Jenny headed over to the art studio after lunch. Their second-to-last meal as free women, Jenny couldn't help thinking. The weekend already loomed over her like a death sentence. It was one weekend, but still . . . she'd been looking forward to spending some time with Easy and to avoiding her room a little more. Now it looked like she and Callie would be in nice close quarters for more than forty-eight hours. *That* sounded like a party waiting to happen. "It seems so weird to just punish everyone arbitrarily like that. Isn't that what dictators do?"

Jenny resisted saying something sarcastic. Alison, still a

card-carrying member of Café Society and welcome at all Tinsley-orchestrated events, had definitely gotten a couple of beers out of the roof party. Jenny and Brett had been nowhere near it. But regardless, it seemed like an awfully harsh punishment to throw on everyone just because a bunch of trustees were going to be in town. "How did a keg even get up there?"

"Dunno." Alison paused to pick a crumbling yellow oak leaf from the heel of her red leather moccasins. "But I did hear that Heath Ferro was planning some sort of big party this weekend."

"How could he have a party without us?" It was a well-known fact that the girls of Dumbarton were the hottest on campus. Or at least they acted like they were, Jenny had noticed. Not that she minded—if felt kind of good to think of herself as hot for once instead of getting all bogged down in the specifics. Like short legs, frizzy hair, boobs that didn't fit with the rest of your body, slight stomach pudge, etc.

"That's what I'm saying." Alison sighed heavily as the girls turned a corner and caught sight of the art building in front of them. "Looks like someone's waiting for you." She nudged Jenny in the ribs, right in a ticklish spot. Jenny squirmed away—she was disastrously ticklish.

Easy was leaning against one of the concrete columns at the entrance to the building. Instead of capitals at the tops of the columns, there were gaps. They were, as the pretty brunette guide had announced to Jenny and her dad on their tour, "ironic" columns. Rufus, who had never heard a pun he didn't like, had laughed so hard Jenny was afraid he'd give himself an aneurysm. Easy's sketchbook was open on his lap. He looked up and gave the two girls a little salute.

"Jesus," Alison murmured under her breath. "You are so freaking lucky."

Jenny couldn't disagree. She could feel Easy's gaze on her as they approached, taking in her tightish cranberry American Apparel crew neck, dark A-line denim skirt (vintage Gap) with a long slit up the middle, and knee-high brown suede Camper boots. Nothing too exciting, but the thing about Easy was that just one look from him—one of *those* looks—and she felt like Cinderella dressed in the most beautiful gown.

"Did you hear the news?" Alison asked Easy as the two girls reached the bottom step, even though he still had his eyes on Jenny. "We're all under house arrest this weekend."

Easy dragged his eyes over to Alison as Jenny sat down next to him and he casually draped his arm around her shoulders. "I heard something about that. Is it true?" He gave Jenny's shoulders a little squeeze and her heart began to pound even harder.

Alison met Jenny's eyes and gave her a quick wink as she headed for the door. "Unfortunately."

Jenny tapped her fingers against the edge of Easy's sketchbook, open to a giant pencil drawing of an oak tree that, instead of leaves, was sprouting squirrels. "Yeah, it's for real." Jenny shook her head. She hoped Easy didn't notice that in all this humid weather, she had run out of defrizz cream and was now sporting an electroshock look. It was definitely a ponytail day, but she hadn't been able to find a hair band anywhere.

"For the whole weekend?"

"Starting at curfew tonight." Jenny glanced at her watch. They still had a few minutes before class, and it was so nice sitting like this, with Easy, on the steps, watching everyone meandering to class on a Friday afternoon, talking about plans for the weekend. Everyone except for the girls of Dumbarton, that is. "It's totally unfair, but they're worried about the trustees and don't want to have to deal with keeping their eye on us, I guess. At least we can still go riding and have a dinner date."

Easy cleared his throat, and Jenny could feel him stiffen a little. Was it something she said? "About that . . ." Easy turned toward her. "My dad's coming up for the trustee meetings, and I sort of have to have dinner with him tonight." His navy blue eyes looked all worried, and Jenny felt bad for him—her dad was totally embarrassing, but she'd never dread eating dinner with him. She actually kind of missed it. "So I guess we'll have to postpone our date until next weekend."

"Hey, no problem." Jenny impulsively gave him a quick kiss on his cheek. "I understand."

"You do?"

"Of course."

Easy shook his head in amazement. "You are so freaking sweet, you know that?"

"I'm just sorry your dad stresses you out so much." Jenny shrugged her small shoulders. "But at least you'll get away from the dining halls for a meal."

"And maybe have some wine, if he's feeling generous." Easy took one of Jenny's curls and started to twirl it around his index finger. "And, oh, five or six lectures."

Jenny giggled. "About what?"

Easy composed his handsome face into a "fatherly" expression. "Too much time on art. Too much time riding." He ticked down a finger with each reason. "Not enough time on serious study. Not enough time thinking about the future. Not enough green leafy vegetables." He folded down his pinky finger and made a fist. "Et cetera, et cetera."

"If it's any consolation, I'll probably be in my room studying while you're enjoying your glass of wine. So it could be worse."

Easy gave Jenny a long look before sliding his pencil stub behind his ear. "You're right." He bit his lip, still looking nervous. Poor, sweet Easy! She wished she could go with him—maybe it would help him feel a little more comfortable if he knew he had someone to back him up. But she didn't want to offer in case it was something he just wanted to get over alone and as soon as possible. Like going to the dentist.

Jenny glanced at the door. "We should probably go in," she said, reluctantly getting to her feet.

Easy followed her slowly, but before he picked up his bag, he grabbed Jenny's arm and leaned in, pressing his lips to her forehead. She closed her eyes, enjoying the moment and the feeling of Easy's lips on her skin.

If only she could freeze this moment and keep on living it forever. Or better yet, kidnap Easy so she could have him with her during lockdown all weekend. Wouldn't a responsible Owl take responsibility for her own happiness?

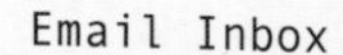

To: JeremiahMortimer@stlucius.edu
From: BrettMesserschmidt@waverly.edu
Date: Friday, October 4, 1:18 p.m.
Subject: ARGH!!!

Jeremiah,

The worst, most horrible, most earth-shatteringly unfair news ever—because of a keg party that Tinsley Megabitch Carmichael threw on the roof last night—how stupid can you be?—the whole dorm got busted and we're all under house arrest this weekend. Now I've been put in charge of collecting essays from all the girls about how to be a responsible Owl. Fuck it. I'm nearly ready to quit DC in protest.

I am so, so sorry I'm going to have to miss your homecoming game—you know how sexy I think it is when you're destroying the other team. I'm bummed about missing out on dinner with the fam and I was looking forward to celebrating with you later too. Alone.

But maybe we can sneak some time in soon somehow?

Love you,

Brett

Instant Message Inbox

HeathFerro: URGENT

TinsleyCarmichael: Speak, HF. Don't just waste my time.

HeathFerro: Meow! Kitty, just need your help getting the kegs from the girl next door tonight.

TinsleyCarmichael: My help?

HeathFerro: Buchanan, his daddy, and McCafferty will be dining with Marymount tonight at 8—perfect opp for us to sneak out the goods.

HeathFerro: Consider it penance for the keg you ladies tapped.

HeathFerro: HELLOW??????

Instant Message Inbox

TinsleyCarmichael: B, I hear you and Julian are dining with the dean 2nite.

BrandonBuchanan: Yup. What's it to you?

TinsleyCarmichael: Just wanted you to know I'm willing to show up to add some more X chromosomes to the mix.

BrandonBuchanan: Uh, thanks, but not necessary. I'm sure all us Ys will get along fine.

TinsleyCarmichael: Never hurts conversation to add a pretty girl to the mix. Don't worry, you don't need me to ask twice. I'll be there at 8.

BrandonBuchanan: Whatever.

Instant Message Inbox

TinsleyCarmichael: Sorry, HF. Won't be around at dinner, so guess you won't be able to get those kegs . . . ttfn

HeathFerro: Don't even start w/me.

HeathFerro: UR joking, right?

HeathFerro: Get back here!!!

A WAVERLY OWL IS ALWAYS FASHIONABLY LATE.

Le Petit Coq, the lone fancy restaurant in all of downtown Rhinecliff, was in an unassuming two-story farmhouse near the far end of Main Street, a house someone's grandmother might live in. Because the town's other dining options included a couple of pizza places, a deli where all the sandwiches were named after dead celebrities, an Indian restaurant the size of a closet, and a Subway, Le Petit Coq was the restaurant of choice for parental visits. Waverly students rarely went there on their own, so it was always a treat to go when parents were in town—your own or someone else's.

"Stop looking so nervous." Tinsley nudged Callie in the side as they approached the steps to the restaurant. Through the gauzy curtains on the windows, the shadowy figures of well-dressed women and men in dark blazers were visible at the candlelit tables. "You're not the one having dinner with the dean."

"You're not the one having dinner with your ex-boyfriend—and his father!" Callie countered, pausing on the bottom step to straighten the two tortoiseshell clips that held the sides of her hair back even though they were already straight.

"True." Tinsley was wearing a black silk georgette Agnes B. shirt-dress, unbuttoned halfway down the front to allow just the right amount of skin to peek out. An ivory cashmere Loro Piana shawl was wound expertly around her shoulders. She tapped the toes of her Fendi patent leather stilettos. "But that's no excuse for being late."

Callie took in a deep breath of the cool evening air and wrapped her arms around herself. She looked perfectly elegant in a plaid pencil skirt and matching cranberry Moschino Cheap & Chic top with a keyhole opening and tie around her neck that she kept playing with. But she was definitely nervous.

Tinsley sighed. She knew this was a big deal for Callie. They hadn't actually talked about it, but Callie had to be secretly hoping that this dinner was the first step to getting Easy back. And for once, Tinsley didn't have much advice to offer. Easy had to know he was complicating things by inviting Callie out to an expensive, intimate dinner with his father. And not mentioning it to Jenny? What was wrong with that boy? It almost made her like him even more. . . .

Tinsley grabbed Callie's hand as she was about to start biting her fingernails. "You look fabulous, honey. You're going to dazzle them." She gave Callie a quick kiss on her cheek and squeezed her damp hand.

"You go in . . . I'm just going to stand out here for another minute and collect myself." Callie gave her a quick smile. "Somehow I know you're going to enjoy yourself."

Tinsley stepped into the vestibule and scanned the first dining area for her dinner companions. As expected, at 8:05 on the Friday night of Trustee Weekend, the place was packed. A gray-haired maitre d' with a fake French accent asked who she might be looking for, and she followed him to her table. The floors were slightly crooked and creaked whenever you moved, but the walls were covered with deep red brocade wallpaper that looked like something Marie Antoinette might have had in her bedroom, and the whole first floor was made up of a dozen small rooms that had been turned into dining areas, creating intimate, quirky spaces. It was a little stuffy—gilded gold mirrors in the bathrooms, the scent of lilac heavy in the air—but Tinsley loved it.

"Voilà, mademoiselle!" the waiter said as he presented Tinsley to the small round table where Mr. Buchanan, Dean Marymount, Brandon, and Julian were already seated. They stood to greet her.

"I'm sorry I'm late." The maitre d' pulled out the empty chair between Julian and Mr. Buchanan and Tinsley slid into the space, enjoying the feel of so many male eyes on her. Mr. Buchanan looked exactly as she imagined Brandon would look in thirty years—handsome and tan and fit, like he managed to cram in a few tough sets of tennis every afternoon between high-powered business meetings, his light brown hair thinning slightly at the temples, a platinum Rolex on his right wrist. He wore a sleek gray Armani suit over a slate blue silk shirt—no tie, the top button undone.

Tinsley held out her hand to him. "Tinsley Carmichael. It's a pleasure to meet you, Mr. Buchanan." He shook Tinsley's hand with the confidence of an older man who has a hot young wife—she'd heard that he'd met Brandon's stepmom while she was still in college.

"We're very pleased you could join us tonight, Tinsley." His brilliant green eyes crinkled at the corners, and Tinsley thought she detected a touch of flirtatiousness. "It's always much more pleasant to have a beautiful face at the table."

Tinsley smiled. Of course it was. "Thank you. It was very nice of Brandon to invite me."

Brandon cleared his throat and shot Tinsley a quizzical look, as if he still was trying to figure out what the hell she was doing there. "My pleasure, Tinsley."

"Thank you, Brandon." She smiled sweetly at him, her pale pink Cargo lip gloss in Bella Bella making her feel more innocent than normal. "And Dean Marymount. It's nice to see you off campus again too." Graciously she held out her hand to the dean, who was wearing, of course, his maroon Waverly blazer and the same Van Gogh tie he'd worn to the DC meeting that morning. It was one thing on campus, but in public? His face colored a little as they shook hands, and he was clearly remembering how Tinsley had caught him, wearing only a robe, with Pardee on the balcony of a Boston hotel less than two weeks ago. Or maybe it was the fact that Tinsley had been nearly naked herself.

Her eyes, at long last, rested on the person she'd been dying to check out the moment she walked in. Julian. Standing next to her, by far the most interesting character at the table. His blondish brown hair was damp and smelled like—something nice. She couldn't figure out *what* without taking a giant sniff. And she didn't want him to know she cared.

"Hi, Julian," she found herself saying, almost shyly, a funny feeling forming in the pit of her stomach. It was kind of crazy, but whenever she met his buttery brown eyes, she felt like they just saw right down to her bones, cutting through all the clothes and skin and bullshit. Did he do that with everyone or was it just her? It gave her the chills.

"You look very nice tonight, Tinsley." He smiled at her politely, but she noticed for the first time that he had a dimple to the left of his mouth that seemed to wink at her.

"Thank you. Please, everyone sit down." Tinsley scooted her chair into the table, noting that there wasn't a bottle of wine in sight yet. It was probably too much to hope that Marymount would allow them to drink in his presence.

"We were just talking about what lovely weather we're having today." Mr. Buchanan closed his menu and clasped his hands. "Perhaps you can help us find a more interesting topic to discuss? Tell me, what are your plans for the weekend? There must be parties and dates and shopping, no?"

Tinsley glanced quickly at Dean Marymount, whose face turned pale. She waited for him to say something, but he gave no indication of wanting to speak up, so Tinsley assumed he'd prefer to keep the lockdown of Dumbarton quiet. "Well," she said, taking her time and enjoying the discomfort on

Marymount's face, "there are any number of things Waverly Owls can do on weekends."

"Do you really refer to yourselves as Waverly Owls?" Mr. Buchanan leaned in conspiratorially.

"Only when trustees are present," Julian quipped, causing everyone to chuckle.

"Don't you have one of your Cinephiles meetings this weekend, Tinsley?" Brandon asked casually, leaning one elbow on the table. His eyes flashed wickedly.

"That has been postponed. Thanks for asking, though." She kicked his foot under the table.

Mr. Buchanan grabbed one of the freshly baked rolls from the basket in the center of the table. "What's the Cinephiles? That doesn't sound like something that was around in my day."

"Your day was a long time ago, Collin," Marymount said, a bit stiffly, like he'd forgotten exactly how to make a joke. Tinsley laughed politely anyway.

"Cinephiles is our film club, started mostly to take advantage of the incredible film equipment the school has. And the incredibly comfortable chairs in the screening room." Her family had donated all of it, but she didn't need to mention that. Chances were, Mr. Buchanan already knew. "We watch movies a few times a month and hold discussions afterward."

"Really?" Julian asked, sounding genuinely interested. He was wearing a pale blue Ben Sherman button-down, and Tinsley could vaguely discern the words MASSIVE ATTACK bleeding through the T-shirt beneath it. "That's so cool. I didn't know Waverly had a film club."

"Tinsley started it," Brandon pointed out, very kindly, she thought.

"We were supposed to watch *Rosencrantz and Guildenstern Are Dead*, but that's going to be next weekend's feature now." Tinsley took a sip of her water (no ice—this really was a French restaurant). "Everyone has a lot of homework this weekend." That had to be true, right? She wasn't about to blatantly lie in front of Marymount, even for his sake.

"Heads. Heads. Heads. Heads. Heads. Heads," Julian intoned, and Tinsley and Brandon both burst out laughing. Marymount and Mr. Buchanan both seemed bewildered.

"It's from the movie," Tinsley explained.

"I can't say that I've ever seen it." Dean Marymount took a gulp of water, a giant drop of condensation sliding down onto the tablecloth with a plop.

"Oh!" Tinsley's eyes lit up. "It's wonderful. It's the film version of a Tom Stoppard play about the existentialist misadventures of—"

"I apologize for interrupting a beautiful girl," Mr. Buchanan interrupted. "But a conversation about existentialism is always improved by the presence of a bottle of wine." He waved over the waiter and pointed at something on the wine list. Tinsley winked at Brandon across the table. And he said his father wasn't any fun.

Julian touched her foot with his. Or maybe he was just stretching. Tinsley kept her foot where it was.

With wine involved, things could only get better from there.

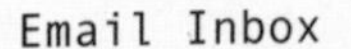

To: BrettMesserschmidt@waverly.edu
From: JeremiahMortimer@stlucius.edu
Date: Friday, October 4, 8:01 p.m.
Subject: Next weekend

Hey, Gorgeous,

That completely sucks about your weekend . . . locked up like Rapunzel? I just wish I'd been at the DC meeting to kick the shit out of Marymount. I'll be thinking about you nonstop.

I'm sorry you won't be able to come out, but don't stress about it. My parents will catch you some other time, and I certainly will too—next weekend, I'll take you out for the most perfect, most romantic date you could ever imagine.

I'm going to crash early tonight but will call mañana. . . .

Love ya,

Jeremiah

P.S. Be a good Owl . . .

A WAVERLY OWL KNOWS THAT A BEAUTIFUL DINNER GUEST CAN BE AN EXCELLENT DISTRACTION FROM AWKWARD CONVERSATION.

Easy sat at the small, slightly crooked table with his father, wishing he were anywhere else but at this overpriced, pretentious Euro-trash restaurant. He picked up one of the thirty-seven forks at his place setting and twirled it in his fingers, willing it to turn into a cigarette. Mr. Walsh gave his full attention to the menu in front of him. He had always been an imposing figure when Easy was growing up—almost six-four, broad-shouldered, deep-voiced, and now, with his gray head of hair and belly that looked like he'd filled it with Kentucky barbecue brisket every day for the last twenty years, he was even more intimidating.

Easy sighed. Where the hell was Callie? He'd seen Tinsley peek into the dining room, looking excited about something.

Maybe she was on a date with another Waverly teacher. But at least five minutes—or fifty—had gone by since then. He really hoped Callie hadn't bailed.

As if reading Easy's thoughts, one of his dad's least attractive skills, Mr. Walsh said, "I certainly hope your girlfriend isn't standing us up."

"She'll be here, Dad." Easy glanced up as their waitress poured water into their heavy crystal glasses. "And she's not my girlfriend." If his dad were a little more human, he'd actually try and tell him about Jenny . . . but Mr. Walsh had a way of trivializing everything Easy felt strongly about, and he didn't want to share Jenny with him yet. But maybe it was totally messed up that he was having dinner with his father and not even bringing up the new girl in his life. Or inviting her to dinner.

Screw that. Jenny was worth more to him than any trivializing bullshit his dad could throw at him. He shifted in his seat and leaned forward. "Actually, I'm kind of . . ."

"Hi." Easy heard a soft familiar voice behind him. He turned around. Standing beside his chair was Callie, looking pale and a little frail, with a nervous smile on her face. She looked pretty in a slim-fitting plaid skirt and dark red top with girlish puffed sleeves. Her blond hair was pulled back from her face, and if she was wearing makeup, it was totally invisible. "Am I late?"

Easy and his dad both stood up. "What a sight for sore eyes!" Mr. Walsh immediately flipped on the charm switch and gave Callie a quick kiss on each cheek. "It's wonderful to see you again, Miss Callie Vernon."

"The pleasure is all mine, Mr. Walsh." Almost immediately, it was like Callie's nervous shell dropped away. She gave Easy a wink over his dad's shoulder, and he couldn't help smiling. "It was nice of you to invite me."

"Please do me the honor of calling me J. L. It keeps me young."

Without thinking, Easy followed his dad's lead and stepped over to Callie himself. "You look . . . uh . . ." He quickly leaned in and gave her a peck on the cheek. He could feel the heat rushing to his face. Suddenly *he* was nervous. "Good."

"I think I need to teach my son how to give a lady a compliment." Mr. Walsh chuckled as they all took their seats. "Callie, my dear, you look absolutely lovely. Doesn't she, Easy?"

Easy cleared his throat, and Callie smiled at him and cocked her head, as if she didn't expect him to answer. "Yes," he said, blushing hotly. "She does."

They began to chat about classes and sports, and Easy listened in awe. Mr. Walsh wasn't exactly the easiest person to talk to—once he sniffed out someone's opinion on something, he started to argue the opposite. But Callie seemed to actually enjoy talking with his dad, and the combination of Callie's contrary nature and her natural southern charm soothed them all. Easy had never really seen her "on" like this before, or if he had, he hadn't been paying attention. It was kind of impressive. The last time Easy's parents had been in town, he'd been too stressed to deal and had stayed tipsy most of the time. But he did remember his parents talking about what a perfect daughter she would make. And it was refreshing to hear Callie talk about something other than which pair of five-hundred-dollar pumps she scored at Barneys. She sounded so smart. It was kind of sexy.

"Callie, I wish you would keep a closer eye on this kid here," Mr. Walsh said, taking a large sip from his glass of cabernet. "I bet an intelligent young lady like yourself doesn't neglect all her academic courses for something as silly as drawing or riding horses." He paused slightly on the word "drawing," letting it fall from his mouth like an insult.

Easy felt his face heat up with anger. Why did his father have to be such a prick? "You know, Dad, there's more to life than getting A's and defending rich, guilty criminals for a lot of money." He thought about telling his dad about the sketch he had hanging in the student gallery but decided against it.

Mr. Walsh laughed. He never seemed to get rattled no matter what Easy said. "Those who have never made money in their life don't have the luxury of criticizing those of us who work for it. I'm only suggesting that if you spent as much time on the rest of your courses as you do on your 'art'"—he made quotation marks in the air as he said "art," as if it was questionable to call it that—"maybe your academic standing wouldn't be constantly in jeopardy."

"You know," Callie spoke up, skillfully pretending not to notice how pissed off Easy was getting, "they say that spending creative energy on one thing often leads to expanded mental capacities overall." A slip of her blond hair fell from her clip and slid down the side of her face.

"Do they?" his dad responded, feigning interest.

Easy looked at Callie in surprise. She and his dad had been chatting and joking around like best buddies, and here she was, standing up to him when he was doing what he loved most—slamming his son? That was pretty brave of her.

And sweet.

"Yes." She set down her fork, which she had been using to poke at her endive salad with walnuts and Roquefort disinterestedly. "Look at all the inventors of the world. Weren't they successful because their minds work differently?" She paused and tugged at the pearl drop earring hanging from her left lobe. "I mean, da Vinci was a great artist *and* a technological genius."

Mr. Walsh took the liberty of pouring another glass of wine for himself, pouring half glasses for Easy and Callie. Easy took his eagerly, not exactly sure what to feel. His father took a sip and gazed appreciatively at Callie "I never thought of it that way, my dear. But I suppose you have a point."

"Besides," Callie added softly, holding her glass of wine to her lips. "Easy's art is really good." She glanced at Easy. "He's very, um, talented."

Easy stared at his plate of half-eaten *terrine des filets de sole*. The weird feeling he'd had before in his stomach had spread throughout his whole body. Callie was being so sweet and protective of him. She'd handled his father like a woman beyond her years. It was as if the past few months of her bitchiness and nagging and needling him had been a dream and he was seeing the Callie he knew before all that, the Callie he'd fallen in love with last year.

Was that what he wanted? The past few months to be erased? That would mean he'd never have met Jenny . . . never have kissed her sweet face.

He couldn't quite imagine that. But as he glanced up at Callie and saw her warm hazel eyes smiling at him shyly, he couldn't keep his thoughts straight at all.

Email Inbox

To: Dumbarton Residents
From: DeanMarymount@waverly.edu
Time: Friday, October 4, 9:30 p.m.
Subject: Lockdown

Dumbarton Residents,

Please note that lockdown begins now. All residents should be in the dorm and are barred from leaving, short of emergency, until Monday morning at 7:00 a.m.

Brett Messerschmidt will be in charge of collecting everyone's essays on what it means to be a responsible Waverly Owl. Please email her directly with any questions.

Your dormitory adviser, Mrs. Pardee, will be mostly absent from the dorm this weekend as her presence is required at the trustee events. However, I assume you understand that anyone who violates the lockdown will be expelled.

Dean Marymount

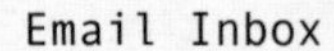

To: Dumbarton Residents
From: BrettMesserschmidt@waverly.edu
Time: Friday, October 4, 9:40 p.m.
Subject: Breakfast meeting

Girls,

Tomorrow morning at 9:00 a.m.—mandatory breakfast meeting in the downstairs common room. (None of us should have any problem getting up that early since it looks like tonight we'll all be trapped in our rooms giving ourselves facials and getting plenty of beauty sleep.)

We have to discuss this essay.

BM

A WAVERLY OWL LISTENS TO SUGGESTIONS FROM HER PEERS.

Saturday morning at 9:03, Brett Messerschmidt was surprised to see the Dumbarton common room full of girls. She'd half expected everyone to blow off her "mandatory" meeting, but maybe everyone had been so bored last night that they were actually grateful for the chance to get together and complain about it. Dining services had dropped off several large boxes of freshly baked bagels and muffins, individual packets of butter and cream cheese, plastic knives, and jugs of orange juice. No coffee, though. Brett could feel her caffeine withdrawal headache already blossoming in her brain. Most of the other girls were still in their pajamas, as if this was some giant breakfast-in-bed treat. It was funny, but Brett didn't even recognize some of them. There were only one or two girls actually dressed. One of them was the Girl in Black, as she and Jenny always called her—the pretty, quiet girl with shoulder-length light brown hair and enormous greenish brown eyes, who always carried a book. She was sitting in the window seat now reading a comic book, wearing a black Bob Dylan concert tee and a pair of black jeans. Brett didn't even know she lived in their dorm.

With a sigh, she grabbed an already-cut everything bagel and a packet of light cream cheese and sat down in an empty armchair in the corner. She couldn't help being in a foul mood. The whole thing was ridiculous—today was St. Lucius's homecoming game, and she was supposed to be in the stands, looking cute and cheering Jeremiah on and making all the St. Lucius cheerleaders know that they weren't going to be the ones going home with him after the game. It was Jeremiah's big day, and she wanted to be there for him. She'd almost fucked things up for good between them, with the whole thinking she was in love with Eric Dalton fiasco, but now things were good again, and she wanted to prove how much she loved him.

Surprisingly, Tinsley and Callie were already seated on one of the couches, Tinsley with her legs draped over an arm. She was wearing a tight-fitting Arizona Wildcats T-shirt (had she dated someone from Arizona?) and her red silk pajama bottoms, her long dark hair rumpled with bed-head. Callie was wearing a white cotton slip and the two girls were whispering in each other's ears, clearly plotting something as usual.

Brett tore off a piece of her bagel and spread some cream cheese on it.

"Thanks for coming, everyone. I thought it would be a good idea if we all got together and brainstormed a little about this . . . um . . . ridiculous essay bullshit." Oops. Brett wanted to sound professional, but she couldn't help letting her bitterness creep through.

A chorus of voices sprang up. "Sage and I had passes to go into the city today." Emily Jenkins's face sported a victimized expression. "There's a Jovovich-Hawk trunk show at Barneys, and we've been planning this for, like, ever. Maybe I can write about that?"

"Yeah, like Marymount's going to give a shit that you didn't get the hot new minidress of the season," Benny Cunningham scoffed as she picked at her banana nut muffin, clearly miffed that she wasn't invited on the Barneys excursion.

Yvonne Stidder, her corn silk hair pulled into two ponytails, raised her hand tentatively. Brett said patiently, "You don't need to raise your hand, Yvonne. We can all just speak up here."

"Thanks, Brett." Yvonne looked around the room a little nervously, looking small and actually kind of funky in her faded red pajamas with Jetsons cartoons scattered all over them. "I just wanted to say that complaining about what we're missing out on is probably not what Marymount had in mind." She glanced at Emily and Sage and added quickly, "No offense."

"I think Yvonne's right," Jenny spoke up, sitting cross-legged on the floor, wearing a pair of True Religion jeans and a striped Ralph Lauren crewneck tee—Brett knew she wouldn't be wearing her pajamas, as she was always careful not to be seen without a bra on. "I mean, he knows we're missing out on stuff—that's the point of the punishment, right?" She took a deep breath. "But he wants us to learn about responsibility, and responsibility is kind of about taking your punishment, fair or unfair, and dealing with it the best you can, you know?"

Tinsley and Callie burst into giggles, and Jenny's face flushed.

"Callie?" Brett said pointedly. "Do you have something to contribute?"

"Actually," Callie answered, still giggling, "we do have an idea about how to deal with the punishment the best we can."

"Marymount might have found one keg," Tinsley announced regally. "But"—she paused for effect, enjoying the looks of bewilderment on the faces of all the half-awake girls—"he didn't find the other five."

Immediately the room buzzed with excitement. "What are you talking about?" Brett demanded crossly. "There are more? Where?"

"Under Kara's bed," Callie revealed proudly.

More buzz as the girls glanced around, not all of them sure who Kara was. It became clear when the Girl in Black jumped up from the window seat, her pale face red with horror. "You're kidding?"

"Sorry," Tinsley tossed out, not sounding apologetic in the least. "You were in the shower, your door was open, and there's too much shit under my bed." She made it sound almost like it was Kara's fault.

"So you put five kegs in my room without asking?" Kara looked irritated. Brett smiled a little, pleased to see the Girl in Black speak up for herself. She had to be pretty cool to stand up to Tinsley Carmichael in front of a room full of Tinsley wannabes. She liked this girl already.

"They're half kegs, actually," Callie corrected.

Yvonne cleared her throat. "It sounds like this is the perfect opportunity to take advantage of a negative situation—we're all trapped here, and Pardee's not going to be around."

"So, let's have a party!" Celine Colista stood up, her Gap Body short-shorts revealing her super-long legs. She did a little jig. A buzz of excitement rippled through the room.

"Right." Brett sat up straighter in her chair and wished she had a gavel or something to regain control of the room. "So what happens when Pardee walks in and sees a bunch of drunk girls passed out in the common room with five empty kegs?"

"Actually," piped up Rifat Jones, the tall, athletic volleyball captain, "I think I can help." Her parents were rumored to practically be running Wall Street before they took time off to join the Peace Corps and were now teaching people in Ghana how to start their own businesses. Kind of cool. "My boyfriend's one of the students on the Trustee Committee," she explained. Her hair was dark and curly and Natalie Portman *V for Vendetta* short, and her long, dark legs that seemed to go on for a million miles were propped up on the coffee table. "He'll be helping out at the big dinner party at the Marymount's house tonight. He said that every year it goes to, like, early morning, and the trustees and teachers get all wasted and have to stumble home. So . . ."

"So he could call us when Pardee leaves?" Tinsley interrupted.

"Sure." Rifat nodded. "He can give us some advance warning, at least. Then we could just lock up the kegs and dive into bed."

"That rocks. Thanks, Rifat." Tinsley clapped like she'd solved the problem herself. Brett was pretty sure that Tinsley had never spoken to Rifat in her life before now, but suddenly she was her best friend. Why not? Tinsley loved everyone she could use.

"So the party is on? Shall we say, eight o'clock?" Callie hopped up from the couch and stretched out her long, thin body. "Just enough time to pick out my outfit."

"Wait a sec," squeaked Yvonne Stidder. "I just had an idea. What if we all have to wear someone else's clothes to the party tonight—someone that we don't really know? I mean, it'll give us a chance to get to know each other." She shrugged and frowned slightly, as if worried that someone would laugh at her.

"That's a fabulous idea!" Rifat exclaimed excitedly, glancing at Callie and Celine and the other tall girls.

Benny Cunningham rolled her eyes at Callie. But Callie was already searching the room, trying to estimate which girls were the same size as her. As if anyone else was that skinny. Other girls were murmuring in excitement.

Brett sighed. A party was certainly not going to make up for missing Jeremiah's homecoming, but the idea of spending an afternoon pawing through closets full of brand-new clothes was appealing to her. It was sort of like the time she and Callie had spent an entire Sunday cabbing around New York, popping into almost every single vintage clothing store in the city in search of a Chanel slip dress she had spotted while flipping through the library's collection of sixties *Vogue* magazines. They hadn't found a dress like it, but they'd managed to bring home bags and bags of other treasures.

"All right," Brett said, brushing everything bagel crumbs off her lap and hoping there weren't any poppy seeds in her teeth. "Everybody, do some thinking about what it means to be a responsible Owl and send me an email." Maybe they could all just compile their thoughts and make one essay. She crumpled her napkin into her hand. "And leave your closet doors open."

Email Inbox

To: HeathFerro@waverly.edu;
EasyWalsh@waverly.edu;
BrandonBuchanan@waverly.edu;
JulianMcCafferty@waverly.edu;
AlanStGirard@waverly.edu;
RyanReynolds@waverly.edu
From: TinsleyCarmichael@waverly.edu
Date: Saturday, October 5, 10:12 a.m.
Subject: Shhh . . .

Dearest boys,

Just wanted to let you know that we'll be having a party tonight in Dumbarton—thought we should invite you since we'll be using your beer.

Pardee won't be around, but security and groundskeeper Ben will be patrolling the quad to make sure no one comes in or goes out. Be here if you can find a way in—just don't get caught or you will be screwed (and not by us).

Naughtily yours,

T

Email Inbox

To: BrettMesserschmidt@waverly.edu
From: KaraWhalen@waverly.edu
Date: Saturday, October 5, 11:21 a.m.
Subject: What I learned . . .

Is that a responsible Owl might as well go to the first party she's ever been invited to. Especially if the kegs are already in her room!

See you tonight.

K

Email Inbox

To: BrettMesserschmidt@waverly.edu
From: EmilyJenkins@waverly.edu
Date: Saturday, October 5, 12:07 p.m.
Subject: Don't you wish your girlfriend was hot like me?

Okay, I have officially been listening to too much bad music. But what I really wish for is hot CLOTHES for me! I need a cute outfit for the party, stat. Can I come over? I'm already on my way.

E

PS A responsible Owl does not spill beer on her generous dormmate's clothes!

A WAVERLY OWL KNOWS THAT WORKING COOPERATIVELY WITH HIS PEERS IS AN EXCELLENT WAY TO BRING ABOUT NEW AND CREATIVE SOLUTIONS.

At twelve-thirty on Saturday, Waverly's dining hall looked, at first glance, like it always looked—crowded. Anyone who didn't know Waverly well would think that all was normal and right in the world. But those familiar with the school would have noticed a distinct difference—or rather, lack. Namely, all of the Dumbarton girls were missing. Meaning, all of the hot girls were missing. And the aesthetics of the school were certainly suffering because of it.

Not to mention the boys. When Brandon walked in the main doors of the dining hall, he unconsciously scanned the room for Callie's pretty blond head and for Jenny's mess of curls before realizing they weren't going to be there. He sighed heavily and headed for the food lines, grabbing a tray and walking around the massive lineup in front of the buffalo chicken strips. (One of Callie's few indulgences—she was going to be pissed about that.)

"More," Heath Ferro told the poor girl shoveling the strips out onto his plate. "Don't be stingy. I'm a growing boy."

Brandon tried not to gag as he passed his roommate in line and grabbed a bowl of steaming tomato soup. His stomach was still queasy from dinner last night. Or maybe he was queasy from all the flirting Tinsley had done with his dad. Talk about weird. She'd appeared out of nowhere and bewitched all of them, except maybe Julian.

"What's your problem, princess?" Heath asked after his plate had been piled sufficiently high with chicken strips. "Didn't you have fun on your date with Julian last night? He said you looked hot." He snickered.

Brandon rolled his eyes and examined the apples for one without any bruises. Heath was never going to outgrow the homosexuality jokes either. Brandon could already picture him at their fifty-year reunion, still making *Brokeback Mountain* cracks. "Tinsley was there too, jackass, in case you didn't hear." He strolled over to the coolers and grabbed a bottle of orange-raspberry juice. Just saying her name electrified him.

"Jesus. No girls for the whole weekend." Heath followed him back toward the table near the fireplace where some of the other guys were sitting. "How fucked up is that?"

"Very," answered Alan St. Girard between giant slurps of his chocolate milk. "I feel like I'm in *School Ties* or something."

"There are other girls around, you know." Ryan Reynolds sighed, not really believing it.

"Yeah, but no good ones."

"Since when did you differentiate?" Heath peeled open his banana and flicked the peel at Alan, then ducked before Alan's apple core could smack him in the face.

Excellent, thought Brandon. *They're like a bunch of gorillas. Take the girls away and soon they'll start eating each other.*

"I don't know if I can make it through the weekend without getting a glimpse of one of Tinsley's short skirts. She's better than Skinemax." Ryan stuffed his chocolate chip cookie into his mouth whole.

"Think about it. All the hotties trapped inside with our beer?" Heath slapped himself on the forehead. "It's going to be legendary. We *have* to get in there."

"And how do you plan on doing that?" Julian asked. The guys had seemed to forget already that he was a freshman and had accepted him into the fold. Normally, if a freshman wanted to hang out with upperclassmen, he'd have to do their laundry or give them weed or something. But Julian was cool, and all the guys wanted him on their intramural basketball teams for winter, so they'd sort of silently forgiven him for being so young. "We can't exactly knock on the front door."

"Wait wait wait wait wait wait WAIT!" Heath jumped up from his seat, sending his glass of water sploshing over onto Brandon's half-eaten sandwich. "What about the tunnels? Are they real? Does anyone know?"

"What are the tunnels?" Julian leaned forward eagerly. This was a story he hadn't heard.

Alan ran his fingers over his unshaven chin. It looked like a blond Brillo pad. "I thought those were just rumors."

"No, they're real." Brandon picked up his sopped sandwich and tossed it onto Heath's tray. "They were built to go between the dorms and the classrooms back during the cold war or something. . . ."

"It wasn't a war thing—they dug them so the students could avoid this fucking numb-nuts Yankee weather." Easy Walsh spoke up for the first time, having been too busy shoveling chicken strips into his mouth to join the conversation.

Oh, yeah, Mr. Tunnels Expert? Brandon thought. "Well, either way . . . they've been closed up for years."

"Yeah, but my brothers used to talk about breaking into them and hanging out there to drink." Easy shrugged. The collar of his stained white polo shirt was coming apart at the seam. "So there's got to be a way in somehow."

"So you can see J-E-N-N-Y?" Ryan poured half a glass of Sprite into his orange juice and swirled it with a spoon. "If I knew I was getting some of *that* ass, I'd be pretty determined too."

"I think the only ass you'll be getting is your grandma's, so why don't you shut the hell up and go give her a call?"

"Ladies, ladies, please." Heath stood up. "Don't you see? We all need to work together on this. Join forces, combine powers for the greater good."

Brandon rolled his eyes. Heath was always going off on these comic book/superpower tangents; like his life wasn't easy enough already, he had to think of himself as some sort of superhero. Although the only power he'd want would be X-ray vision so he could see through girls' clothes.

"Whatever," Ryan grumbled. "I mean, I'm in."

Easy tossed his crumpled-up napkin on Ryan's tray as a peace offering. "So let's figure it out. . . . How do we even find the tunnels?"

"Teamwork, ladies, teamwork." Heath pounded the table with his fist. "We all go our separate ways. Someone take the library, Maxwell Hall, the art studios, Lasell, everything. Leave no stone unturned. No door or trapdoor unopened!" It was like he thought he was Professor Xavier making a speech to inspire all the X-Men before going into battle.

"What if it's locked?" Brandon asked.

"What?"

"What if the unopened door is locked? Then what?"

Heath looked at his roommate as if he were a five-year-old who had just asked the stupidest question he'd ever heard. "Then we make like *Oceans 11* and pick it."

And since all the girls were gone, they'd have to shoplift some hairpins.

Email Inbox

To: JennyHumphrey@waverly.edu
From: EasyWalsh@waverly.edu
Date: Saturday, October 5, 1:12 p.m.
Subject: Picnics

Jenny,

I miss you. Have no fear, the mighty Heath Ferro has a plan. We're going to try and sneak in—we can have our dinner date in your room instead of the woods.

Luv,

E

Instant Message Inbox

CallieVernon: Hey, Walsh. Please thank the big guy for a lovely dinner last night.

EasyWalsh: He'd probably dig it if you sent him an email yourself—you know he's in love with you.

CallieVernon: Ha ha ha . . . Yeah, it was surprisingly fun. J. L. Walsh is like a fine wine—he gets better with age.

EasyWalsh: Depends on your definition of better. At least no food was thrown.

CallieVernon: You sneaking in tonight with the rest of the guys? I hear there's a secret plan.

EasyWalsh: Ferro is acting as our fearless leader, so you know we're in good hands.

CallieVernon: As long as you make it . . . we girls are all dressing up, hoping some sexy knights in shining armor will break down the doors. . . .

EasyWalsh: Um, yeah. We'll try.

A WAVERLY OWL KNOWS WHO HER DORMMATES ARE—IN CASE IT COMES IN HANDY.

After delivering gourmet sandwiches for lunch (turkey and Havarti on croissants, portobello and goat cheese on flat bread), dining services must have needed an easy one since they announced that for dinner, they would be ordering a giant stack of pizza boxes. No one seemed to mind. In fact, pizza was Tinsley's favorite meal before a big night of drinking. Nothing like carbs and cheese to prep the stomach for alcohol.

All afternoon, the girls had left the doors to their rooms—and closets—open, and everyone roamed around the floors, pawing through racks of clothes that weren't even their size, just in case they saw something spectacular. Tinsley had been through Benny and Sage and Celine's closets, and she knew Callie's like the back of her hand, but everything seemed boring. Dry. Conventional. Unsurprising. Her wardrobe had been picked clean by dozens of hands. She didn't mind sharing, as long as she got outfits as good as she gave.

Brett came storming into the room, an emerald green chiffon garment hanging over her arm. She didn't even glance at Tinsley as she tossed the dress onto her bed. She clicked on her Harmon Kardon stereo, flooding the room with the sound of Fleetwood Mac. Could Brett be any lamer? Who liked seventies music besides the people who were actually alive in the seventies?

With a glare at Brett that was meant to be withering, Tinsley left the room, slamming the door behind her.

She sighed. Five-thirty—the boys, if they managed to find a way in, would be here in a couple of hours. She might as well check on the beer—the kegs probably needed new ice. Never before had the ice machine in Dumbarton's basement seemed so essential.

Kara's door was the only closed one on the whole floor. Tinsley knocked briefly before twisting the knob. Kara was sitting at her desk, books open in front of her. "Hello?" Tinsley called out.

Kara spun around in her chair. "Oh . . . hey." She didn't look happy that Tinsley was there. *Please.* Tinsley was doing this nobody girl a fucking favor, allowing her to store the party refreshments in her room. No one even knew who she was before today. She could at least show a little gratitude.

"Just wanted to check on the kegs—you don't mind if we leave them here, do you?" Tinsley glanced around the spotless, tidy room. "It's just so clean in here. And no one would suspect you."

Kara dropped her arm over the back of her chair. She was

still wearing the Bob Dylan T-shirt she'd had on earlier. Hopeless. "Yeah, whatever." Her greenish brown eyes met Tinsley's violety blue ones.

Tinsley crouched near the bed and lifted the bedspread out of the way. She pressed one of her hands to the metal of the keg. Cool enough. She stood back up. All right, she could be a little nicer to this girl—after all, she hadn't exactly asked her before she'd stored the kegs in her room. "How come you're not dressed?" Tinsley inquired. "You're coming to the party, right?"

"Well . . ."

"Oh, come on!" Tinsley straightened up and for the first time glanced at Kara's open closet door. With the eye of a shopping aficionado, she took in the bright colors and expensive fabrics. Wait a second, whose stuff was this? The girl who wore only black had a closetful of clothes like *these*? In two quick strides, Tinsley was in front of the closet, pulling at a gorgeous dusty rose dress with a pleated waist and full, swingy silhouette. It looked like something out of the twenties. She held it up against her body. "Where did you get this stuff?" she exclaimed, already eagerly pawing at the other things.

Kara's chair squeaked as she pushed it back across the hardwood floor. She walked timidly toward Tinsley. Tinsley considered herself an expert on body language, and she could tell Kara didn't trust her. Tinsley looked at her more closely. She was one of those girls you don't realize is pretty until you've been looking at her for a few moments, and suddenly, like a jigsaw puzzle, the pieces fall into place. Her shoulder-length hair was stick-straight, a mild, honey-tinted brown, and she was small and curvy. She still had some baby fat on her face, nothing that a little skilled makeup application couldn't turn to her advantage, and gorgeous, wide-set greenish brown eyes that were completely wasted on someone who didn't know how to use a touch of eyeliner.

"My mom." Kara watched as Tinsley pulled out a pair of white satin sailor pants and squinted at the tag. Frannie Oz. "She's . . .um . . . a designer."

Tinsley's jaw dropped. "Are you kidding? She made all these? You lucky bitch."

Kara shrugged, completely oblivious to what a freaking gold mine she was hiding in her closet. "She went a little overboard this year—she sent me all these samples from her spring line."

Tinsley spun around and rubbed her forehead. "So why on earth are you not wearing them?" She was careful to avoid criticizing the Bob Dylan T-shirt and black jeans—some girls were so sensitive. But *this* girl had such a soft face that the all-black look was totally overwhelming.

"I don't know." Kara sighed and ran a hand through her shaggy graham-cracker-colored layers. She could use a haircut too, Tinsley decided. Something short and clipped to help make her face look less round. "I mean, I don't know if they'd even fit me."

She was clearly insane. "That's why you try them on, dummy." Tinsley tugged a burnt-orange scarf-like spaghetti-strapped wrap dress, with an uneven hemline and a delicate paisley pattern (there was even some black in it to satisfy her goth tendencies), and forced it into Kara's hands. "Here."

"It's really not me. . . . It won't look good."

"Do me a favor and try it on." Tinsley pointedly turned her back and continued to rummage through the closet. There were some amazing things in there—although Tinsley had never heard of the label, she'd be on the lookout for it from now on. All the designs had a vintage flavor to them, and the funky prints made Tinsley feel like she'd stumbled into the perfect little unknown boutique. Too bad Kara's mom wasn't the one living in this room—Tinsley would hire her to custom-make her some clothes! "If you've never worn it before, it counts as borrowing something."

A few moments of uncomfortable silence passed as Tinsley listened to the rustling sounds of Kara changing her clothes. "Done yet?" she asked, after enough time had passed. She spun around.

Kara stood in the middle of the room, tugging at various parts of the dress, which fit her like a glove. The skirt swirled out a little at the bottom, a few inches above the knees, and the deep V-neck revealed just the right amount of Kara's curvy chest. "It's too tight. I feel like a hooker."

Tinsley giggled. "Now I know you're insane." She stepped forward and tucked the label back beneath the fabric. "You look sexy. You are *so* not allowed to change. That's what you're wearing tonight."

Kara sighed again. "Well, uh, thanks." She looked a little surprised when she checked out her image in the mirror on the back of her door. "I suppose I'm going to have to wear some makeup too, right?"

"As long as you're doing it, you might as well do it right."

"I guess."

"Why don't you come over to my room?" Tinsley offered generously, still clutching the rose chiffon dress that looked almost like a peignoir Maggie would wear in *Cat on a Hot Tin Roof*. "Have you met Brett before? I mean, you're new here, right?"

"Not exactly . . ." Kara's cheeks turned pink. "I mean, I haven't really met Brett yet." She cleared her throat and started fussing with the neckline of her dress. "Maybe I'll come over in a little bit. I've got to figure out what to do about shoes."

Tinsley held up the dress she was carrying. "You don't mind if I try this on, do you?" Kara was a little curvier than she was, but the dress had a tieback waist.

Kara waved her off. "Help yourself."

Tinsley smiled. If there was one thing she knew how to do, it was help herself.

She stepped out into the hallway and saw Callie, her fist raised and about to knock on Tinsley and Brett's door. Her hair was damp from the shower, and she was still wearing her thick white Egyptian towel wrapped around her body. "Is the pizza here yet?" she demanded, her eyes flashing. Callie must be really hungry to be asking about food—usually she kind of pretended that she didn't need to eat. But . . . there was this sort of impish look on Callie's face today.

Tinsley grinned at her old friend. "Smells like it. Let's grab some slices."

"Wanna bring them upstairs and do our makeup? I think Jenny's going down to your room."

Already forgetting about the makeup plan with Kara, Tinsley nodded. "Absolutely."

Email Inbox

To: HeathFerro@waverly.edu; AlanStGirard@waverly.edu; EasyWalsh@waverly.edu; RyanReynolds@waverly.edu; JulianMcCafferty@waverly.edu; LonBaruzza@waverly.edu
From: BrandonBuchanan@waverly.edu
Date: Saturday, October 5, 5:47 p.m.
Subject: Tunneling to paradise

Gents,

Problem solved. We have an in.

Meet at 7:25 at Lasell gym, boys' locker room. Come prepared for underground travel. Think stealth.

Don't be late. And if anyone owns a headlamp—please bring with!

B

To: BrettMesserschmidt@waverly.edu
From: BennyCunningham@waverly.edu
Date: Saturday, October 5, 6:00 p.m.
Subject: A penny saved is a penny earned

As I languished in my dorm room today, bored out of my mind and dejected at the thought of missing a to-die-for sale, I had an epiphany that changed everything: a responsible Owl should appreciate the lack of temptation provided by mandatory dorm lockdown. My not being allowed to use my wallet really paid off in the end because if you think about it, 500 dollars saved on a few shirts I'll wear once is 500 dollars in my pocket. To be used for more practical purposes, of course.

By my calculations, that's about 125 handles of Absolut. Did I mention staying in your dorm all day long helps sharpen math skills? I feel so enlightened!

Smooches,

Benny

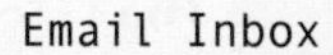

To: BrettMesserschmidt@waverly.edu
From: JennyHumphrey@waverly.edu
Date: Saturday, October 5, 6:17 p.m.
Subject: Cheer up!

Brett,

Smile, sweetie. There's a party tonight!

I've been finding my hair bands all over the room, like someone took my Altoids box of them and flung them all into the air. Weird, right? Being a responsible Owl means not murdering your roommate, no matter how much she drives you insane.

So, are you wearing that green dress of Rifat's? Want to get ready together? Wherever our roomies are not?

See you in a few!

Jenny

IT IS COMMON COURTESY FOR A WAVERLY OWL TO KNOCK BEFORE ENTERING.

Brett was lying on her bed in Rifat's ABS emerald silk halter dress, looking like a Hollywood starlet reading *Catcher in the Rye*. She was technically ready for the party, but after pawing through dozens of other girls' closets, finding the most amazing dress, and borrowing an incredible pair of gold Giuseppe Zanotti sandals with Grecian ties that wound around her calves, she still didn't feel like partying. She just wanted to be with Jeremiah.

She hadn't heard from him that morning, but she'd managed to tune her clock radio in to the St. Lucius radio station, and she'd listened to the student announcers give a play-by-play of the game. It was clear that they were both in awe of Jeremiah, which had made Brett giggle, and it was fun to hear about all the amazing passes he threw, like he was saving the world from nuclear annihilation instead of throwing a ball. The game went down to the last few seconds, when Jeremiah managed to run into the end zone himself to score the game-winning touchdown. The nerdy announcers went ballistic, and the cheerleaders probably swarmed the field, pom-poms wagging.

Sigh.

But *Catcher in the Rye* always managed to make her feel a little better. Brett loved the whole book, but the first few chapters were her favorite. Holden Caulfield was such a train wreck, and so clearly out of place at his expensive prep school, that Brett was certain she was in love with him, at least a little. The part where he says that sometimes, after finishing a certain kind of book, he always wanted to call up the author—that was something Brett felt every time she read Salinger or Dorothy Parker. She wanted to call Salinger up and tell him how much she felt like Holden sometimes but that she disguised it better.

A gentle knock at the door ripped Brett from her reverie. "Come in," she called. The door opened slightly and Kara peeked in, looking gorgeous in a snugly fit burnt orange mod dress.

"I didn't mean to bother you if you're reading," the girl said, clearly a little flustered. "But . . . Tinsley said to come over and she'd give me a hand with my makeup. I'm completely inept at it." She glanced around the room. "But I see she's not here."

Brett closed her book and set it next to her on the bed. "Well, I think she might have gone up to Callie's room, but I can help you if you want." She stood up. "I'm no Tinsley, though," she added.

Kara bit her lip. "I'm not sure if that's a bad thing," she said with a nervous laugh.

Brett giggled. "Excellent."

Kara's eyes fell on *The Catcher in the Rye*. "Great book—are you reading it for English?"

"No." Brett glanced down at the pretty white book, its cover blank except for the title in black in the middle and some minimalist rainbow stripes that shot diagonally across the corner. She loved that too. "I guess I just read it when I'm depressed."

Kara nodded wisely, her greenish brown eyes widening with sympathy. "Holden's such a fuckup," she said fondly. "He always makes you feel better."

Exactly. Brett couldn't imagine why she'd never met this girl before. "That's an awesome dress, by the way."

"I can't believe you're saying that to *me*!" Kara exclaimed. "You look like a movie star."

"I don't look like a zucchini?" Brett glanced down at her dress as she headed over to the makeup tray on top of her dresser. She picked up her Global Goddess tube of concealer and held it out for Kara. "This stuff is amazing."

"No one is going to mistake you for a vegetable."

"Thanks." Brett examined Kara's face critically. She had nice skin, strong cheekbones, and incredibly long lashes—she never wore makeup, so it might be nice to give her face a little more color. "How do you feel about lilac eye shadow?"

Ten minutes later, Jenny peeked her head in the door; she was wearing a beachy strapless J.Crew dress in a dark espresso and a pair of strappy red sandals. "I don't look too out of season, do I?" Her hair hung in damp ringlets across her bare shoulders. "I just loved the way this dress squashes down my boobs." She thrust them forward. "They look smaller, don't they?"

"Not when you do that," Brett teased. Easy wasn't going to be the only one all over her tonight. Even though her dress wasn't revealing, the bare shoulders and deep, shadowy V of her cleavage were going to drive all the boys wild. Brett examined her own face in her mini–makeup mirror before dusting a teensy bit of Urban Decay Oil Slick dark shadow at the corners of her eyes.

Jenny checked out both of them. "You both look fantastic." She smiled shyly at Kara. "You're Kara, right? I think I'm in your Human Figure Drawing class."

"It's such a great class," Kara gushed. "As long as I don't have to pose anytime soon."

"Maybe if we got to wear these clothes, it would be fun." Jenny twirled around and let the skirt spin out in a circle around her.

"I think I'm gonna change. Not my makeup," Kara added quickly. "But this dress is so not me."

"But that's the point of wearing different clothes—you don't have to be yourself tonight," Jenny pointed out, looking in the mirror and twisting strands of hair near her forehead and clipping them back in the center of her mass of dark curls.

"Maybe." Kara shrugged. "But I don't like looking in the mirror and not recognizing myself, you know?"

From outside came a strange honking sound, almost like the horn Brett used to have on her pink Huffy bicycle. The girls dashed to the window, and Brett pulled up the shades.

"What the hell was that?" Jenny asked nervously. "It sounded like something dying. Owls don't sound like that, do they?"

"Only when they're on crack," Kara joked. "That must have been a goose."

Brett stared out into the darkening evening but couldn't see anything other than bushes and trees. Another call came, this time closer, and the three girls jumped. Brett's heart started to beat faster and she pushed up the window and stuck her head out.

"Oh my God," she shrieked. Jeremiah, dressed in black with two stripes of black reflector paint beneath his eyes, was wedged between the brick wall of Dumbarton and an overgrown lilac bush.

"Shhh . . ." he whispered, putting his hands on the windowsill. "Aren't you going to invite me in?"

Giggling and feeling like a complete rebel, Brett grabbed one of Jeremiah's strong hands and helped him through the window. "Aren't you supposed to be at dinner with your parents?" she demanded happily.

Jeremiah shook his red hair, letting loose a flurry of pine needles. "We had an early one." He glanced at the other girls and pointed at Jenny. "Hey, Jenny, right?"

"Yeah." She glanced at Brett nervously. "How'd you know?"

"You've got some fans." He grinned his irresistible grin at her.

"Aww," Jenny replied, blushing.

Brett grinned. Jeremiah was such a flirt. One of the benefits to having a boyfriend who went to a different school was that Brett could innocently flirt with as many guys as she wanted and never have to worry about Jeremiah knowing. Flirting was one of those things that made life worth living. The disadvantage, of course, was realizing that Jeremiah was probably doing the same at his school.

"I'm glad you could . . . uh . . . make it this evening." Jenny giggled.

Brett nudged Jenny with her elbow. "And this is Kara."

"Hey, Kara. Nice to meet you. I'm Jeremiah." Brett smiled. Jeremiah was polite as always, even when his fingers were covered with sap.

"Nice to meet you too, Jeremiah." Kara smiled back and grabbed Jenny's arm. "We were just, um, leaving."

"Yes. Of course!" Jenny motioned toward the door and the two of them backed out it, giggling still. "But we'll see you at the party, right?"

"We'll be there in a few," Brett said. She could still hear her heart pounding in her ears. All day, she'd been too afraid to hope that Jeremiah would sneak over—she didn't want to get him in trouble or anything, but she couldn't stop thinking about him. As soon as the door was closed, she threw her arms around him and started kissing his face wildly, being careful to avoid the black smeary stuff.

"Whoa, slow down a sec." Jeremiah rubbed his hands up and down Brett's sides. "Let me get a chance to see how gorgeous you look." He stepped back and appraised her, and Brett felt her whole body heating up. "Wow."

"I like a man of few words." Brett pulled him to her again and this time pressed her lips squarely against his. Their bodies seemed to melt together as he tightened his hold around her waist. "Congratulations on the game today. I listened on the radio."

"Oh, yeah?" Jeremiah placed one hand on the nape of Brett's neck and massaged it gently, exactly where she liked it. "That's sweet of you."

"Mmm." Brett pressed her face into his chest and breathed in. He smelled like pine and fresh deodorant and the AXE shaving cream he always used. Having him here, in the flesh, after wanting him so badly all day, made Brett feel a little like she was in a dream. She couldn't help herself from unbuttoning the top button of his black Ralph Lauren shirt.

"Babe, what are you doing?" Jeremiah murmured in her ear, not exactly sounding alarmed.

"I can't help it. . . ." Brett tore the next few open a little faster, the glimpse of his bare chest driving her wild. There were so many buttons! "I've been dying to see you." She finally pulled open his shirt and was greeted with the words, in bright body paint, GET GOOSED, St. Lucius's slogan. "Oh my God."

Jeremiah grinned sheepishly. "Yeah . . . uh . . . all the guys painted our chests. We didn't realize that it doesn't really come off in the shower." He scratched his fingers across his pecs.

"You're kidding?" Even the silly slogan on his chest made him look sexy, and she slowly leaned in and pressed her lips to it, tracing the first G with her mouth as she slid Jeremiah's shirt off his arms. Maybe this was something she and Jeremiah could always have between them—knowing that the first time they did it, his chest said GET GOOSED in big red, goofy letters. That was kind of romantic.

But just as she started to push Jeremiah toward the bed, the door popped open and Tinsley, wearing a flowy pink dress and a long double strand of freshwater pearls—exactly like the ones Brett had been planning on wearing out with Jeremiah's family—barged in. "Oh, Jeremiah! I didn't expect to find *you* here." As if she was expecting Brett to be with some *other* guy.

Considering it was only a few short weeks ago that Brett was sneaking onto Eric Dalton's yacht, Brett felt stung. *You passive-aggressive wench*, Brett cursed. Couldn't Tinsley just let things go? Jeremiah glanced at Brett, and she could see in his blue-green eyes a touch of sadness, like Tinsley had just reminded him of the horrible way Brett had dumped him not all that long ago. Brett rubbed her hand up and down Jeremiah's bare back.

But Jeremiah grabbed his shirt off the floor, giving Brett a quick kiss on the cheek and mouthing the word "Later."

Tinsley strode right past Jeremiah's half-naked body and gave him her sparkly smile. "Congrats on the win. I heard it was a really good game."

"Thanks, Tinsley."

Brett glared at Tinsley as she fumbled around with a few things on her desk before grabbing her sleek black phone, humming the whole time.

"You guys hanging in here all night?" Tinsley asked brightly, looking directly at Brett, as if she hadn't not spoken to her for the past two weeks. Tinsley never wanted to reveal her true megabitch self in front of members of the opposite sex.

“No, we’ll be out there, don’t worry,” Brett replied, keeping the nastiness she was feeling out of her voice. Jeremiah pulled on his shirt.

“Good,” Tinsley said, leaving the door open behind her. “I wouldn’t want you to miss anything.”

A WAVERLY OWL KNOWS WHEN TO CONFIDE IN HER ROOMMATE AND WHEN TO KEEP QUIET.

On the second-floor landing, Jenny pressed her body against the wall to allow Celine Colista and Verena Arneval, who shared a room down the hall in Dumbarton 309, to pass. Verena, who Jenny had never seen in anything other than elegant dresses and heels, was looking like a club girl in a pair of skintight black leather pants and a white tuxedo-inspired Badgley Mischka halter top, and Celine, who loved anything formfitting, looked classy in a turquoise long-sleeved, off-the-shoulder blouson dress and a pair of off-white ballet flats.

"Hey, Jenny! You look great in my dress," Verena cried as she and Celine flew down the stairs in a fit of giggles. "But you're going the wrong way! The party's in the lounge!"

Jenny wasn't used to wearing a strapless dress—she thought they'd just slide down below her boobs, exposing their enormousness to the world. But she'd splurged last week on an expensive strapless bustier bra that promised to lift up as it squeezed in, and it actually seemed to work. She even felt kind of sexy. "Just, um, gotta brush my teeth." Jenny smiled awkwardly at the two girls, who disappeared down the stairs with their tan arms playfully linked.

Suddenly Jenny missed having Brett as a roommate, and she missed even more being on friendly terms with Callie. Not that they'd ever exactly been there. From the very beginning, Callie had merely tolerated her until suddenly she became useful, and only then was she half nice to her. But Jenny didn't care—she knew Callie wasn't really as cold as Tinsley, and she felt like they might have ended up being really good friends if the Easy thing hadn't come between them. Was it completely naive to think that Callie would eventually get over that?

Back in her room, Jenny felt even lonelier—and the room wasn't even empty. Callie was standing in front of the mirror, applying mascara. A pair of Rock & Republic jeans hung loosely around her hips, as if she hadn't been able to find anyone with clothes small enough to fit her, and though they bagged a little around her nonexistent butt, she looked fabulous. On top, she wore a sheer white cami with tiny pink rosebuds from Betsey Johnson, and her newly short hair was pulled back into two stubby pigtails.

Callie turned around, the open mascara wand in her hand. Her eyes were lined thick olive, and her lips were covered with clear gloss. She looked like the epitome of the California girl—thin, natural, and playful. She'd never looked prettier.

Callie smiled nervously at Jenny. "I'm not, like, insane for wearing jeans, am I?" She fumbled with the zipper, making sure it was flat. "I know everyone's wearing, like, evening gowns and looking fabulous . . . like you do," she added. "But I tried these on from this girl Ashleigh? Down the hall? And they just felt so good." She paused to catch her breath.

Whoa, Jenny thought. *I guess after being silent for so long, Callie finally had something to say*. She certainly wasn't going to let that opportunity pass. "I think you look awesome," Jenny gushed, because she really did. "You look like Cameron Diaz."

"Well, I'm glad I don't have her acne problem," Callie answered wryly, reaching for a gold bangle bracelet on the top of her dresser. She glanced over her bare shoulder at Jenny.

"She has an acne problem?" Jenny asked curiously.

"You didn't know that?" Callie seemed surprised, as if everyone knew about Cameron's acne woes. But then she softened a little. "Yeah, it must totally suck. When she gets nervous, her entire, like, face breaks out." Callie opened a tiny pot of lip gloss. "It's why she doesn't go to premieres."

"Oh." Jenny was grateful that flawless skin ran in her family. Not being able to go to premieres would kind of suck, especially if you were famous.

"Everything okay with you?" Callie glanced over her shoulder. "You seem kind of . . . out of it."

Callie Vernon was asking her how she was feeling? Two hours ago the girl wasn't speaking to her, and now she was sharing celebrity gossip and acting all concerned about why Jenny was quiet? But maybe that was Callie's way of getting over things—one day she woke up and moved on? Or maybe she met a new guy? "Well . . ." Jenny hesitated, trailing off.

"Is it Easy?" Callie asked softly, kneeling down by the stack of new shoe boxes, searching for the right pair. She bit her lip. "I mean, look. I'm sorry I've been kind of . . . a bitch." She glanced up and Jenny was surprised to see she actually was blushing. "It's just been, you know, kind of weird."

"Hey." Jenny felt something heavy in her throat. "You don't need to say anything. I completely understand." She could see that Callie was uncomfortable apologizing, and even if the last few weeks had been *more* than uncomfortable, Jenny was still the one with Easy. She could afford to be generous. "*Really*."

Callie glanced up at Jenny and gave her an incomprehensible look, then grinned. "Okay." She pulled a gold Calvin Klein collection ankle strap sandal from the top box. "Too fancy?"

Jenny cocked her head. "No. I think it's a perfect balance to the jeans."

Callie collapsed on the bed and started tugging on the shoes. "You can talk to me, you know. I won't bite."

Feeling a rush of roommate love, Jenny had the urge to spill everything to Callie. "Well . . . it's just that he said he might try to sneak in tonight. But I haven't heard from him all day."

Callie nodded sympathetically. "He can be bad about those things. He was always standing me up or showing up like an hour late. It's totally frustrating."

"It's just kind of nice to know what's going on, you know?"

"Yeah. But when he was growing up, his parents were super-strict and made him tell them whenever he was going somewhere, exactly where he was going, and when exactly he would be back." She held out her right foot and waggled it back and forth, examining how it looked from different angles. "By the time he got here, I think he just couldn't deal with that anymore, and now it's sort of impossible for him to be on time or tell anyone where he is."

"Oh." That answer was an unavoidable reminder of the enormity of Callie and Easy's relationship. It was like pulling a tooth—at first, it looks kind of tiny, but then you see how far and deep the roots go back. Jenny and Easy were just starting to know each other, but Callie had been a part of his life a lot longer. "I guess I didn't realize all that."

"I'm sure he'll be here," Callie said, deliberately not mentioning that Easy had also IM'd her that he'd be sneaking in tonight. "He'll find a way to get in." There was no way Easy would miss out on something as legendary as sneaking into the girls' dorm when it was on lockdown. Please.

Jenny unzipped her pink Sephora travel bag and spread her makeup in front of her. Callie watched as she opened her Benefit Dandelion highlighting powder and brushed a little bit onto her face, making her skin look even more radiant than usual. In that deep brown strapless chiffon dress, with her long, wild curls, she looked like someone who would frolic barefoot in a wildflower meadow and not worry about stepping on bugs. In other words, the kind of carefree girl Easy would fall in love with.

"I guess you're right. I really can't imagine Heath letting all of us girls get dressed up and drink his beer without him."

Jenny closed one eye and swept her wand of clear mascara over her already-long lashes, her mouth opening as a reflex. Her hand was right above her Altoids tin of hair bands, which was—shit—half full again. So she must have realized that Callie flung them all over the room?

Callie suddenly started to feel like a bad person, and not just because of the hair bands. Jenny looked so innocent and vulnerable that Callie started to have regrets about going out to dinner with Easy and his dad last night. Maybe it wasn't the smartest move for anyone involved? Her tongue felt heavy in her mouth, and she wondered if she should just tell Jenny about it while they were being open about all things Easy.

But she couldn't. She had told Easy that she wouldn't, and even though she felt bad about it, she kind of liked having a special secret with him.

"I think I'm going to go up to the roof and get some air." The room felt crowded, and Callie needed to get away from Jenny, whose sweetness only made her feel more and more guilty. "I'll, uh, see you downstairs."

Callie opened the door and the sound of the Red Hot Chili Peppers wafted up the stairwell.

At least *someone* was having fun.

A WAVERLY OWL KNOWS THAT EVERY DOOR HAS A KEY.

At seven twenty-five sharp, five minutes before closing time, the boys had all congregated in the locker room at Lasell gym. And waited.

"I don't know if I should be doing this," Lon Baruzza said as he locked the front door of the gym and switched off the last of the overhead lights. "But I miss all the hot girls." He jangled the keys and grinned. "And it serves 'em right for making me lock up every freaking Saturday night."

Brandon grinned, feeling much more daring than he usually allowed. He'd been hanging around the squash courts this afternoon, practicing his backhand, when Lon Baruzza walked by with a stack of fresh towels for the boys' locker room. Brandon saw him working everywhere—in the dining hall, the library, Maxwell—doing all sorts of odd jobs for his work-study program. Brandon had always admired him for that—there weren't too many kids at Waverly, himself included, who knew what it was like to have to work for their first-class educations. But this time, Brandon was admiring him for a different reason: the enormous set of keys hanging from a belt loop on his dark wash Abercrombie & Fitch jeans.

"I don't have a master key or anything that cool," Lon admitted when Brandon asked him. "But there are a bunch of old keys on here that open a lot of strange doors. And yeah, one of them opens the Lasell access door to the tunnels." He shrugged.

"How the fuck did you keep that a secret?" Brandon swiped at a bead of sweat running down his forehead.

"Well." Lon grinned proudly. "It's not exactly a secret—a few girls know about it too." Lon was reputedly a ladies' man, although he wasn't one of the guys that talked about it much. Or emailed lists of all the girls he'd hooked up with out to his dormmates. In other words, he was no Heath Ferro.

"Do you know how far they go?"

"I haven't really explored them. But they have signs on the walls—apparently they go to all the main buildings."

"Dorms included?"

Lon nodded. "Dorms included."

Bingo.

Brandon filled in the stealth group of explorers by email, though even he wasn't sure what he meant by "come prepared." Flashlights and dark clothes, maybe. But then Walsh showed up wearing a yellow hard hat with a giant light on the front of it.

"Spelunking." Easy shrugged and set it on his head. He looked like a miner. If the girls were here, they'd be falling all over themselves trying to tell him how cute he looked. How *creative* and *artsy* it was that he was wearing a fucking *spelunking* helmet. Brandon just thought he looked like a dweeb.

Alan St. Girard started pulling a thick rope from his bag and wrapped it around his waist.

"Fuck's that for?" Ryan Reynolds asked, stroking his nose ring and looking a little self-conscious about the tiny LED penlight he'd brought.

"In case anyone needs pulling out."

"Whoa." Heath Ferro held up a hand. "No one needs to be talking about pulling out. Yikes."

"These aren't caves, you know." Brandon pulled on a black V-neck Armani sweater over his faded gray Ben Sherman T-shirt. He glanced at Julian, who had hung what appeared to be binoculars around his neck. "Binoculars?"

"Night vision goggles," Julian corrected. His hair, normally flying all over the place, was sticking out the bottom of his black knit cap. He looked like a really tall Kurt Cobain—maybe it was a Seattle thing.

"Lemme see." Heath Ferro grabbed at them, but Julian, about six inches taller, pulled them off his neck and held them above his head.

"I don't trust you with expensive toys."

"Where'd you get those?" Brandon asked, curious. This Julian kid was an enigma. "My mom." He held them up to his eyes and pretended to focus on Brandon. "She was CIA."

"Really!?" Ryan Reynolds jumped up and down with excitement. Everyone knew *Alias* was his favorite show.

"No." Julian smiled.

"Fucker," Ryan mumbled.

Brandon tapped his black Camper bowling sneaker impatiently against the linoleum floor. "Are we ready? The girls are waiting."

Lon led them to the basement of the old gym building, where the ceilings were low and all sorts of outdated gym equipment was stored. He stopped suddenly in front of an innocuous-looking door, right next to the football coach's dingy office. He flicked through his keys expertly before sliding one into the lock and twisting it back and forth. Everyone held their breath. Someone hummed, "Dum da dum dum DUM!"

The door opened with ease. "Lon, I love you. Let's go!" Heath clapped and grabbed his flashlight from his pocket. He shone it on the walls, illuminating a sign that looked like a directory. He paused at the name Dumbarton. "Ladies, here we come."

Easy clicked on his spelunking light, and Brandon hated to admit it was incredibly helpful in lighting the way. Still, the tunnel was much wider, more navigable, and less Edgar Allan Poe–esque than Brandon had expected.

"This way." Julian pointed, the other hand holding his night vision binoculars to his eyes. Where the fuck did you get something like that? Brandon started to think that maybe Julian's mother *was* in the CIA after all.

"This rocks!" Alan exclaimed when they came to the first turnoff that led to the library. "Why would anyone deal with the fucking snow in winter if they could be all warm and snuggly down here?"

"Maybe that was the problem." Brandon's flashlight slid over some writing scratched across the walls—*Madison Oliver gives good head, I Masterful Johnson, Taylor loves Michael 4 ever, Duran Duran rocks my world.* Guess Waverly Owls had never been terribly creative with their graffiti. Brandon shone his light on one: *Marymount has a teeny weeny.* He nudged Heath in the ribs. "Sounds like you guys should be buddies."

Heath glowered, still pissed about Jenny's impromptu revenge cheer about his body parts at homecoming last month. He grabbed the rope from Alan's hand and swung it around in front of him like a lasso. "You can't believe everything you hear, dickwad. You'll probably be too busy trying to get into Callie's pants tonight to notice, but I'm going to be the belle of the fucking ball. Again."

At the mention of Callie's name, Brandon felt nothing—something that, in itself, was monumental. His heart didn't beat faster, he didn't start picturing her in her white Shoshanna bikini with the tiny little cherries on it, he didn't start wondering what guy might be drooling over her at the moment. It was pretty fucking amazing.

And terrifying. Because it was Tinsley he was picturing in that bikini.

"Uh, yeah, whatever." Brandon tried to clear his thoughts, but suddenly they were filled with images of Tinsley. He had been thinking about her a lot since dinner last night, but so far he'd managed to convince himself that he was just shocked to see her behave like a normal, albeit ridiculously flirty, human being. But now that they were getting closer to Dumbarton, he realized that he was kind of excited to see Tinsley again. Maybe he'd been wrong about her. Maybe she wasn't evil but just . . . um . . . misunderstood?

"Baby doll! Are you still not over that girl yet?" Heath trilled, unable to let the Callie thing go. He probably didn't ever want Brandon to get over her because then he'd have to find some new material.

"Get off his back," Easy called over his shoulder as he led the way up front with Julian. "It's not his fault. Callie's a great girl. She'd make a lasting impression on any guy."

Collectively the boys dropped their mouths. *She'd make a lasting impression on any guy*? Like, *Easy*? Brandon couldn't help being irritated with Easy, not only for pseudo–standing up for him—no, thanks, dude—but for waxing sentimental about Callie. Maybe it was just paranoid-jealous Brandon returning, but it sounded like Easy was still into her.

Which pissed Brandon off to no end. First Easy breaks Callie's heart—now he was going to do the same to poor, sweet Jenny? Jenny, who was unbelievable—who was almost perfect in every way except for her exceedingly poor taste in guys. Admittedly, the image of her nearly busting the seams of that cherry bikini top had also played a part in a few of Brandon's daydreams.

"Wait wait wait wait wait wait waiiiiiiiiiiiiiiiiiiiiiiiiit a second, cowboy." Heath stepped in front of Easy and put a hand on his chest. "Aren't you supposed to be with little Miss

Bouncy right now? Isn't she supposed to be the one making *impressions* on you?" He made a lewd gesture of pressing his chest into Easy's body.

"Get off me, jackass." Easy slapped Heath's hand away. The two of them stared each other down.

But thankfully, before there could be a lot of macho shoving and shouting, a loud thumping noise came from up ahead. "Guys," Julian called back. "This is it." Immediately everyone crowded around him, their flashlights focused on a small doorknob. Above it, in unmistakable lettering, was the word *Dumbarton*. Julian turned the knob and pushed.

Nothing happened.

He turned and pushed again; this time Heath slammed his body against the door too. It flew open, sending both of them tumbling out, knocking over a bucket and mop.

Julian gazed up at the ceiling, and everyone was silent as they listened to the sound of "Like a Prayer" coming from somewhere above their heads. "Holy mother." He stood up and adjusted himself. "We're here."

Heath Ferro held up his compass. "Let me get my bearings," he said, sniffing the air. "The beer is . . . this way!" He pointed toward the door out of the storage closet—the only door.

"Nice work, Nancy Drew." Brandon rolled his eyes. "Let's go."

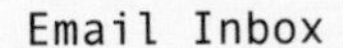

To: BrettMesserschmidt@waverly.edu
From: YvonneStidder@waverly.edu
Date: Saturday, October 5, 8:00 p.m.
Subject: Rock on

As much as it sucked being cooped up all day long today, I am SO happy that us girls are bonding the way we should be, and it is totally unfair that we are being punished for it. A responsible Owl works hard to establish and preserve friendships with fellow students. I mean, there are schools that don't even allow boys at all because they so value female connection, and here we are just trying to hang out with our girls and we're getting, like, imprisoned for it! But like I said, I'm just happy we got time together. Can't wait for tonight!

Lovin' my sisters,

Yvonne

Instant Message Inbox

BennyCunningham: At long last, the boys have arrived! Where are you, baby?

CallieVernon: I'm on the roof, smoking cloves. . . . R all the boys there?

BennyCunningham: U mean, is EZ here?

CallieVernon: That's not what I meant. But is he?

BennyCunningham: Yup. And looking reeeeeeeeeeeally cute.

CallieVernon: Great.

BennyCunningham: If your ass isn't down here in three minutes, I'll drag it down!

Instant Message Inbox

VerenaArneval: Chica, where are you?

JennyHumphrey: Just sending an email to my dad . . . I'll be down soon.

VerenaArneval: Your father surely doesn't expect you to write when there's a party heating up.

JennyHumphrey: I'm sure he'd be quite happy to have me staying in my room all night.

VerenaArneval: Not when there's a certain tall, dark, and handsome cowboy looking for you . . .

JennyHumphrey: Sold! I'll be down in two minutes.

VerenaArneval: Hurry, or I might jump him myself!

A WAVERLY OWL KNOWS HOW TO TAKE CONSTRUCTIVE CRITICISM.

In a well-intentioned but probably not all that convincing move, the girls of Dumbarton had decided to spread all their textbooks and notebooks around the downstairs common room just in case Angelica Pardee or some other authority figure happened to peek in. In a way, it was more exciting for the boys to see the girls' dorm as it might be any day of the week, not all fancied up. It made it seem more intimate. Easy could imagine Jenny lying on the couch, doing her algebra homework, her little pink sneakers dangling off the edge.

But chasing that image out of his mind was one of Callie, sitting in that window seat, staring at the copy of *Vogue* that she had tucked in the pages of her history book.

What was his *problem*? Why couldn't he get his feelings about these two girls straight in his mind? It wasn't fair to anyone to keep thinking this way about both of them, but he couldn't help it. It was like choosing between Mandy Moore and Lindsay Lohan—he thought he'd made his choice. It was Mandy all the way—if only he could stop thinking about Lindsay.

"Took you guys long enough." Alison Quentin stood in the doorway to the common room, hands on her hips, wearing a simple white tank top with a pair of skinny black cigarette pants and a pair of red skimmers. She looked a little like an Asian Audrey Hepburn. Easy glanced at his roommate Alan, who had an enormous crush on her.

"Did you miss us, honey?" Alan St. Girard grabbed Alison by the waist and spun her around. She giggled but didn't fight it, and the two of them danced down the hallway.

"Kegs are this way," she called over her shoulder.

Easy spotted a box of pizza lying open on the coffee table and grabbed a slice. A few girls he didn't recognize were playing a game of Twister in the corner, and he was sort of impressed. Most of the time, Twister was just an excuse to grope members of the opposite sex. Good for them. Chewing his slice of cold mushroom-and-olive pizza, he headed up the stairs. Even though boys were banned from girls' dorms, except for the common areas in the brief period between sports practice and dinner, Easy knew his way to room 303 blindfolded.

He paused at the door, not sure who he was going to find inside. And not sure who he was hoping to. He knocked gently and pushed open the door.

Miles Davis's "Kind of Blue" was playing, and Jenny was sitting at her desk, typing away at her laptop. He watched her for a moment and listened to the sound of keys clicking. She looked so pretty, her dark brown curls tumbling down over her back.

He tried to sneak over and surprise her, but the floor creaked beneath his Converse high-tops and Jenny whirled around. "You're here!" she cried, her small face breaking out into an enormous smile. "Why didn't you say something?" She quickly sprang out of her chair and walked over to him, looking totally hot in a dark brown strapless dress that matched her eyes and looked like something you'd throw on over a bikini. And she was barefoot. Mmm . . .

Without a word, Easy slid his hand behind her neck and leaned in to kiss her. His heart was thumping so wildly he thought maybe she could hear it, and he suddenly realized it *was* Jenny he wanted to see. And to kiss. Her little round shoulders looked practically edible.

"Wow," Jenny whispered softly after they pulled apart. "What did I do to deserve that?"

Easy flopped down on her bed and stared up at her wide brown eyes that reminded him of the double-fudge brownies his mother would always make for his birthday or whenever he was sick. Jenny looked like she should be running barefoot down the beach, maybe throwing a Frisbee to Easy, a giant black Labrador retriever chasing along after them in the surf. Maybe part of the problem was that he was always having these fantasies—if he could just stay in the moment, maybe he'd be able to figure out what it was that he wanted.

"Just for being you." Easy folded her pillow in half and

placed it under his head, enjoying the orangy smell of the stuff she and Brett put in their hair.

"You're in a good mood." Jenny bounced down on the bed beside him.

"Yeah, well . . . it was kind of an adrenaline rush to sneak in like that." *Not to mention seeing* you, Easy thought.

Her eyes widened. "You didn't, like, parachute in or anything? Did you?"

"No." Easy stroked Jenny's bare arm, the tiny blond hairs almost invisible. "There are these tunnels. Under the campus."

"Like . . . sewers?" Jenny asked, leaning away from him as if he smelled. Which he was pretty sure he didn't.

"No, dummy." Easy grabbed her arm and started planting kisses at her wrist and moving up to her elbow. "They built them in the old days, when students were too chickenshit to walk outside in the snow." Jenny had gorgeous arms—they were tiny because she was tiny but not scrawny and malnourished like Callie's.

"Really? Sort of like subway tunnels." Jenny shivered a little—either from Easy's touch or from being cold. "Did you see any rats?" Or from thinking about rats.

"No rats." *Just a couple of jackasses*, he thought, remembering how he'd almost punched Heath. Easy was normally a complete pacifist, but Heath, with all his insinuations about Callie, had been even more obnoxious than usual.

Or maybe it was because . . . No, couldn't be.

Jenny glanced down at Easy, her smile shy, her pearly white teeth peeking out from behind her ruby lips just a little. "It's nice to have you here. . . . I spent like five hours finishing this annoying algebra problem set. If I have to factor one more trinomial, I might kill someone."

Um, schoolwork. Right. Easy closed his eyes. "Yeah, well, I spent all day avoiding this fucking annoying history assignment Wilde gave me yesterday." Friday morning, Mr. Wilde had sent him an email sharing his less-than-stellar grade on Thursday's test. In fact, he'd flunked it, as predicted. But because Mr. Wilde was one of those stand-up kind of teachers, he'd offered Easy the chance to do a makeup writing assignment over the weekend. He was supposed to write a five-page fictional interview between a news reporter and General George Washington about why he would make an excellent first president of the new country. It was nice of Wilde to give him a second chance and all, but did he have to make it such a cheesy assignment? That was even worse than a regular old boring one.

He rubbed his hand over his eyes and thought of all the hours he had wasted with Alan playing Xbox—like, four. And he'd stayed up late last night working on a series of caricatures he was hoping to work into a big project for his portraiture class, which wasn't actually due until the end of the semester. There were a billion other things he could have—should have—been doing.

"When's it due?" Jenny asked sympathetically, touching one of the curls near Easy's left ear.

"Monday."

"Why's he giving you so little time for it?" Jenny's eyes widened. "Doesn't he know you have other homework too?"

"Well . . ." Easy started. "It's sort of a makeup assignment—I kind of failed this big test on Thursday."

"Oh, no." Jenny looked more upset than if *she* had failed the test, which was kind of sweet. "That sucks."

"Whatever. I'll just whip out some crap tomorrow night. I don't really want to think about it."

Jenny bit her lip, looking worried. "You didn't have to sneak in tonight, you know. We could have seen each other some other time."

Easy was a little hurt. "You didn't want me to come?"

"No!" Jenny placed a small hand on Easy's chest. He could almost feel its warmth through the peeling Chicago Cubs logo. He wondered if she liked going to baseball games—if she'd share a ballpark hot dog with him and not stress about how many calories were in it. "That's not what I meant. I just . . . you know." She shrugged. "You're still on probation from the beginning of the year and everything. I don't want you to get in any more trouble."

Easy tried to smile, but he felt the little hairs on the back of his neck stand up straight. Even though Jenny wasn't saying anything that wasn't true or that he hadn't already thought of, it just sounded sort of . . . irritating. Like his father had somehow enlisted his girlfriend to continue his good work, like he'd asked her to keep an eye out for him. Which, however well intentioned that might be, made him feel *smothered*.

She didn't want him to get into any more trouble, which was nice. But didn't she ever take risks? What if someday Easy wanted to go, say, skydiving? It was something he had always dreamed about—flying through the air! Would Jenny try to talk him out of it or would she strap on a parachute and jump out of the plane holding his hand? He couldn't help wondering if Callie would be up for it. She was a debutante and all and would probably worry about how her hair would look at fifteen thousand feet, but then again, she did have a wild (and somewhat self-destructive) streak.

"I appreciate that. . . ." But . . . how could he say this nicely? "You know, at dinner with my dad," and Callie, he was careful NOT to add, "he just loved talking about all the things I do wrong. So, I sort of don't want to think about it anymore."

Jenny bit her lip. "He's really that hard on you, huh?"

Easy felt himself melting. "Well, it's not like he ever beat me or anything." His mouth twisted into a smile. "So it could be worse. But really, let's talk about something interesting."

"All right." Jenny grinned, and Easy realized he didn't even know if she'd ever had braces. Or pets. Or imaginary friends. He wished there was a way to pause things—make everything in the world stop moving except for the two of them and just lie down together. And talk or not talk. Whatever. They just needed to get to know each other a little better. "So how did you guys get into the tunnels? If people don't use them anymore, aren't they, like, boarded up?"

"I don't know if I'm allowed to reveal our secrets." He stroked his chin like he was deeply conflicted about telling her any more. "But maybe I could be bribed."

"Bribed?" Jenny wrinkled her nose, making the spray of little freckles dance. "I'm afraid I don't have any money."

"That's not a problem." Easy sat up and leaned on his elbow, looking up at her. "There are other ways." As always, he was thinking too much. Maybe he was schizophrenic or something. He tried to ignore the feeling of unease in his stomach and just enjoy the moment. He was here, with Jenny, whose hair was falling into her face as she leaned in to touch her lips to his. He didn't feel like talking anymore.

She pulled away a little quickly after the kiss, almost as if she knew something about it wasn't right. "Why don't I go down and get us a couple of drinks?" She stood up, tugging at the hem of her dress and sliding into a pair of red flip-flops.

"Uh, yeah." Easy flopped back against her pillow and smiled weakly. "That sounds good."

"Okay." She gave him a searching look, and for a moment he wanted to pull her to him and tell her about dinner last night and let her know every single crazy thought that was running through his mind, knowing that she'd put him at ease. But he didn't even know if he'd be able to vocalize them. He wasn't even sure what he was feeling himself; how could he talk about it? And so he just smiled, and Jenny smiled and left the room, and he closed his eyes and wondered if Callie's pillow still smelled the same as he remembered.

A WAVERLY OWL KNOWS THAT TIME DOES NOT HEAL ALL WOUNDS

Jenny started down the wide marble stairs toward Kara's first-floor room, her red J.Crew flip-flops thwacking loudly against the bottoms of her feet. She was feeling a little dazed about what had just happened with Easy—not that she had any idea what had just happened. But for the first time since she'd met him, something just seemed to be off. Things were normal at first, but then, all of a sudden, it was like somehow they weren't speaking the same language or like everything she tried to say just ended up coming out all wrong. It made her nervous.

She was relieved to be out of the room. Maybe she just needed a beer. Jenny didn't exactly like beer—did anyone?—but having one always helped her feel less awkward. And right now, she was positively craving one.

On the first floor, the music was playing at a reasonable

volume, one that would not attract the attention of any teacher or other authority figure that happened to pass. Not like the notorious roof party. Apparently a responsible Owl learns from her mistakes. Sort of. She passed Brett's closed door and heard some soft music playing. At least someone was getting some quality cuddle time!

Just as Jenny approached Kara's doorway, a girl passed through the front hallway that Jenny knew for sure she had never seen before. Her short dark blond hair was pulled back into a ponytail, revealing a black underside—a look more at home on the sidewalks around Union Square than at Waverly Academy. She seemed older too, wearing a long dark skirt and a fitted leather jacket—uh-oh! Was she a new teacher? Some kind of grad student Marymount had hired to infiltrate the dorm? Jenny heard a flutter of activity and a rash of slammed doors—clearly others had spotted the stranger in their midst too. Kara came rushing around the corner, eyes flashing. "Quick, in here." She pulled Jenny into her room and slammed the door behind them.

"Who was that?" Kara asked, looking like she enjoyed the excitement. She'd changed into a white, romantic-looking silk blouse with an empire waist and a square neckline with a little trim of lace that managed to push her chest up and make her look like a Shakespearean heroine. The billowy sleeves were long and sheer, and Kara had paired them with a funky pair of tight black pants that hugged her thighs and flared out at the calves. Her scuffed Doc Martens peeked out from beneath. She still looked hot but way more comfortable than she had in the tight burnt-orange dress. This outfit was just so much more *her*.

"I have no idea." Jenny leaned against Kara's bookcase, which was stacked with books vertically and horizontally, the only messy part of the otherwise immaculate room. "She did look pretty young to be a teacher."

"But why would someone just wander into a girls' dorm?" Kara wondered as she crouched down and filled two plastic cups from the keg under her bed. "Maybe she's just from a different dorm."

Jenny smiled and ran her eyes over the books. It was nice to see so many—most of the girls used their bookshelves as shoe racks. It reminded her of the hours she'd spend at the Strand Bookstore in Greenwich Village, tilting her head to read the titles on the thousands of shelves of books until her neck hurt. She recognized the spines of a couple of her favorites—*Goodbye, Columbus*, by Philip Roth, *Slaughterhouse-Five*, by Kurt Vonnegut, *Pride and Prejudice*, before noticing two entire shelves of thin, colorful spines with small print. She pulled one out a little and saw that it was a vintage copy of an X-Men comic book from 1968. "Oh my God—are these all comics?"

"Yeah, I have sort of an obsession. . . ." Kara blushed. "I know it's a total geek thing—I'm like the Comic Book Guy on the *Simpsons*."

"No!" Jenny protested, pulling out a copy of *Ghost World*, her all-time favorite graphic novel. She loved the seamless way art and words fit together. "I can't believe you have this!"

There was a shuffling noise in the closet before the door

suddenly burst open and Heath Ferro, a black chiffon scarf wrapped around his forehead like a sweatband, stepped out, holding an empty Waverly Owl mug and smelling like beer. His shaggy blond hair was in desperate need of a trim, and he looked a little dazed, as if he had just woken up. "Are you guys talking about comics?"

"Is that my scarf?" Kara lunged for it, but Heath darted away. He crouched down in front of her bookshelves and pulled out about twenty comics.

"Holy *shit*. You have the original X-Mens?" He glanced up at the girls, his green eyes lit up like he had just hit the mother lode. "I can't believe you're into comics!"

"Because I'm a *girl*?" Kara placed a hand on her hip and stuck out her chin defiantly. Jenny took a step backward. Kara could be kind of scary when she was pissed.

"Because you're a *hot* girl!" Heath stood up and held out his right hand in an uncharacteristically polite manner. Jenny remembered that when she'd first met Heath, he'd been unable to look at anything other than her chest. Here he was, trying to be a gentleman? It was unprecedented. "We haven't been properly introduced."

Kara glanced at his hand as if he'd just told her he had the bird flu. "Even though you're wearing my scarf on your head and were hiding in my closet. Funny."

Heath was undeterred. In fact, Kara's attitude just seemed to turn him on all the more. He draped his right arm on the top of the bookshelf as if that had been his plan all along. "I'm Heath."

Kara's look could have cut glass. "I know who you are."

Heath continued to be oblivious while pretending to stretch and scratch his stomach so that he could lift up his T-shirt and show off his chiseled abs. "See, all the new girls have a way of tracking me down. I'm really one of the few guys worth knowing at Waverly, if you like real guys, that is."

Kara was silent, and Jenny could sense that something was wrong, though she had no clue what it might be. There was something weird going on between Kara and Heath—the tension between them was electric, and it looked like Kara wanted to kill him. Either that or kiss him. Even though Heath could be kind of slimy, he wasn't truly offensive. And he was definitely handsome. But Kara kind of looked like a volcano about to blow its top.

"You probably haven't gotten to see too much of the campus yet. At least, not the tunnels." He raised his eyebrows provocatively at Kara, already having forgotten that Jenny was in the room. "We could go *spelunking*."

"You are *unbelievable*." Kara shook her head, her full lips trembling a little. Jenny took a step forward, wondering if she should tell Heath to get out of there before Kara lost it. She was clearly having some sort of allergic reaction to him. "You don't even *recognize* me, do you?"

Heath looked completely floored. "Recognize you?" He closed the X-Men comic he was still holding, set it back on the shelf, and patted the back pockets of his 7 For All Mankind jeans, as if his pack of Camels could help him now. "We didn't already . . .uh . . . hook up, did we?" Jenny could see that all of his "intimate moments" with girls were equally meaningless.

"Not in this lifetime," Kara snapped back. Her cheekbones were flushed and she was clearly one of those people who anger happens to make prettier. She took a deep breath and held her shoulders back straighter. "I was in your English seminar with Miss Dubinsky freshman year? I sat behind you?" Heath's face remained blank. Kara continued. "Kara Whalen? But you had a nickname for me . . ."

"You mean . . ." Heath staggered backward, and Jenny could tell that he was genuinely shocked and not just putting on one of his shows. "You're the Whale?" He puffed his cheeks out like a chipmunk.

Jenny's jaw dropped. It was a thing of beauty, what happened next, and Jenny watched it all as if it was happening in slow motion. Kara, enormous eyes flashing with fury and maybe a teensy bit of satisfaction, picked up her maroon-and-white Waverly mug half filled with warmish beer and, without thinking twice about it, flung it into Heath's handsome face. It was like something that girls do in movies or books but not in real life. And if there weren't a shocked, sopping-wet Heath Ferro standing in front of her, his royal blue Lacoste polo shirt with the alligator torn off dripping little beer droplets onto the perfectly clean hardwood floor, she might not have believed it.

A giggle escaped Jenny's lips—she couldn't help it.

"Once an asshole, always an asshole." Kara glared at Heath. "I had to leave *school* because of people like you, you know. You got *everyone* to call me that. You thought you were so clever and so popular and so charming that making my life a living hell didn't matter at all!"

"That doesn't mean you had to throw your fucking beer at me!" Heath pulled his shirt away from his chest and it made a suction sound. "I mean . . ." He looked pissed, but his eyes ran up and down Kara's body, as if he was trying to figure out how this could be the same person he tormented. "I'm sorry I was mean to you, all right? I don't even really remember it."

"Well, *I* do." Kara gave a small shudder and suddenly she didn't look angry anymore. She looked tired and maybe a little embarrassed. She glanced at Jenny nervously.

"There are paper towels in the bathroom, Heath." Jenny put her hands on her hips and nodded toward the hallway, as if to say, *Get the hell out of here.* The thought of Heath, or anyone, being such a jerk to someone as nice as Kara gave her the shivers. She didn't understand what some people got out of being mean—it was why Tinsley was such a mystery to her.

"You girls are fucked up, you know that?" Heath tried to force a laugh as he flung open the door and stepped into the hallway. "If you wanted me to take off my shirt, you just had to ask." He started to pull it off, but Kara quickly kicked the door shut with her foot.

There was a moment of silence. "Do you think I'm crazy?" Kara asked quietly as she pulled her bath towel from the hook on the back of the door and dropped it on the puddle of beer.

"Are you kidding?" Jenny grabbed a tissue from the box on Kara's desk and wiped at the splattered beer on the wall. "I've been wanting to do that to Heath since I got back here. I'm jealous. Although to be honest, I think it kind of turned him on."

"Gross." Kara's face wrinkled in disgust, but then she smiled. "You're really cool, you know?" She sighed. "I wish you'd been around . . . before."

Jenny wasn't going to press her. "Well, I'm around now." Had Kara really had to leave school because everyone was so nasty to her? Suddenly Jenny's own experience leaving Constance Billard—after a series of highly visible mistakes—seemed much less dramatic. And besides, she'd sort of wanted them all to happen.

"Thank goodness." Kara thumbed the books on her shelf. "I've been sort of hiding out this year. And I never wanted something like that little scene to happen. But now I'm kind of glad that it did."

"I've never seen Heath look uncomfortable before, so you definitely scored points there." Jenny glanced down at her shoes, suddenly remembering Easy, waiting for her up in her room. But she didn't want to rush back right away—it was fun hanging out with Kara.

"Although he's probably going to be walking around without a shirt on for the rest of the night."

"I guess there's a price to pay for everything." Jenny took a big swallow of beer. "Was everyone really mean to you?"

"Not everyone." Kara's eyes looked sad. "Some were nice. But most people just ignored me. God forbid there are Waverly Owls who don't fit into a size six."

"I would have been nice to you," Jenny said, wondering if that was really true. She certainly wouldn't have been mean—but she thought back to her first day at Waverly, when nerdy

Yvonne Stidder was showing her around and trying to get her to join the jazz ensemble. The girl was nice enough, but Jenny couldn't wait to get away from her and meet the cool kids. And since she'd made friends with Brett and Easy and Brandon and all the others, she hadn't given Yvonne a second thought.

I'm a bitch, she thought. *I'm one of them.*

A WAVERLY OWL IS NOT AFRAID OF SKELETONS—LIVING OR OTHERWISE—IN HER CLOSET.

"So, what's it like sharing a room with the girl who stole your boyfriend?" Benny Cunningham asked as she pushed open the door to Dumbarton 303. She made a beeline for Jenny's dresser and snooped through the things on the top of it. She opened a porcelain butterfly-shaped box and picked out a silver chandelier earring disinterestedly, then took the cap off Jenny's bottle of Euphoria by Calvin Klein and spritzed the air.

Callie rolled her eyes and closed the door behind her. Benny could be a bit of a rubbernecker—she loved details about everyone else's problems, which she'd listen to pityingly before offering some completely unwelcome and unhelpful advice. Callie had been having an excellent time alone on the roof, feeling sorry for herself and smoking cloves from the pack she kept in her pajama drawer for special occasions only. She loved the way they made her lips tingle and made her feel all lightheaded, but her asthma kept her from smoking them too often.

But then Benny had snuck up to join her, with a "special" cigarette that Alan St. Girard had rolled for her (courtesy of his parents' "herb" farm in Vermont). Now her mind was all loosened up and wandering and she could feel her emotions rising up inside her and threatening to spill out her mouth.

"It's not that bad." Callie lay down on her own bed and closed her eyes, wishing everyone in the entire world would disappear. That she could be all alone, sprawled out on a sandy tropical beach, the sun beating down on her bare skin, with the sound of waves crashing in her ears instead of Benny Cunningham's insinuating remarks.

"Oh, no?" Benny asked innocently, checking her image in the mirror. She was wearing a Fresh floral thermal top with a multicolored hummingbird emblazoned on the chest and a short white denim miniskirt, borrowed from the closet of some senior girl on the second floor. Her perfectly parted brown hair was pulled into two low Heidi braids, and Callie knew she was going for the whole girl-next-door look. "It certainly looked that way."

"Give me a fucking break." Callie leaned up on her elbows, liking the way the waist of her slim-fitting jeans didn't even touch her stomach. "People don't get stolen away. That's just a convenient myth so that people don't have to blame themselves for problems in their relationships."

Benny turned to check out her ass in the mirror and smiled at her own reflection. "Come on—everyone saw the way she threw herself all over him."

"That's not true."

"Sure, it is. She was after him from day one."

"I asked them to flirt with each other . . . so that I wouldn't get in trouble." That had to be one of the stupidest things she'd ever done. Right up there with making out with Heath Ferro. Twice.

"So what? You asked them to flirt, not fall in love." Benny grabbed Callie's bottle of DuWop lip venom and, without asking, spread it across her plum-colored lips.

Callie shook her head and realized she meant every word she was saying. "You don't get it. Someone can't just come between two people if their relationship is solid." She rubbed her hands over her eyes. "Things weren't right between Easy and me. That's all there is to it."

Benny was unimpressed. "That's awfully mature of you."

She sighed. It had taken a lot for her to get to this point. For so long, she'd been furious with Jenny. It was easy to blame Jenny's perky boobs or sweet personality, but now it just seemed silly. If Easy had still been in love with Callie, no one would have been able to tear him away. And that was the hardest thing to accept. "Whatever. It's hard." She felt her throat filling up with tears. "I miss him."

"Aw, sweetie." Benny spun around. "Do you need a hug?"

Callie moved away from her toward the half-opened window. "Some other time." Benny was really starting to get on her nerves. She needed some new friends. "Why don't you go downstairs? I'll be down in a minute."

"You need to do some more soul-searching?"

"Fuck you!" Callie almost laughed. Benny had a hard time taking things seriously sometimes, especially after smoking. "I've got to change my shoes."

"I'll save you some beer," Benny trilled, then shut the door.

Callie frowned—it was one of those days. Talking about Easy—thinking about Easy—did not make anything easier. She wanted to get over him, she really did. But after dinner on Friday, after the way Easy had been looking at her, she couldn't stop thinking that maybe her second chance was coming? And then his IM—it made her feel like she wasn't imagining things, that maybe Easy didn't exactly have his mind made up either.

She wasn't sure if she was looking forward to seeing him or not. It was all too weird.

But she did know that her feet were already killing her, and no one can be happy with sore feet. She stood up, stumbled over to her closet, and pulled open the door.

"Aieee!" she shrieked, jumping back when a light shot out at her. *What the hell?*

On the floor of her closet, crouched on top of her jumble of shoes and clothing that had slid off the hangers and her bag of dirty laundry, was a person—a person with a yellow plastic helmet on with a blinding flashlight strapped to it. *Easy Walsh.*

"Easy!" she gasped. "What the fuck are you doing in here?" Her mind raced back to all the things she'd been saying to Benny. Not like it was anything to be very embarrassed about now. Still, she felt her face flush.

His ears stuck out a little from beneath his helmet. "Hiding," he whispered. All crouched on the floor like that, with his ridiculous hat perched on his head, he looked like a little kid. Like a five-year-old who'd found the best spot in hide-and-seek and was waiting patiently for someone to discover him.

It wasn't the isolated beach she'd been hoping for, but suddenly there was no place she wanted to be other than the bottom of her own messy closet, with Easy Walsh.

She slid off her towering gold sandals and stepped, barefoot, into the closet, her knees trembling a little. She pulled the door closed behind her, giggling. Easy pushed some clothes away, doing his best to clear a spot for her on the floor. She eased herself down next to him.

"You are such a goof-ass," Callie said as Easy flipped the bird with his hands and his flashlight projected its shadow onto the closed closet door. She laughed, a full, deep laugh from the pit of her stomach. All it took was five seconds with Easy, and she was as happy as she'd ever been.

Easy sniffed the air. "It smells like mothballs in here."

Callie held her hand up to her eyes. "Can you shut that light off? It's kind of blinding."

Easy fumbled around with the helmet for a minute before they were suddenly plunged into darkness. It felt quieter, as if somehow the darkness blanketed out any other noise, too. Callie couldn't even hear the sounds of the party downstairs anymore—just the sound of her own breathing.

And Easy's.

"Hi," he said.

"Hi," she whispered. Then she laughed, and he laughed too. It was all so absurd. Callie felt the hem of a dress tickle her forehead, making her giggle even more. She wanted to pause time and stay in here in the closet with Easy forever, just the two of them, with no one else to get in the way. It was perfect, just like this.

And then they were kissing, and it was even more perfect.

Instant Message Inbox

BennyCunningham: Where the hell'd the party go?

RyanReynolds: Thought a teacher came in? Lon and I are underneath some crazy chick's bed, waiting to be rescued.

BennyCunningham: How cozy . . . can you take a pic?

RyanReynolds: Maybe later, if you join us.

BennyCunningham: A responsible Owl never abandons her fellow Owls.

RyanReynolds: Hallelujah for that.

WAVERLY OWLS TAKE HYGIENE EXTREMELY SERIOUSLY.

When the word spread about a possible teacher infiltration, Tinsley had just been about to approach Brandon and Julian to thank them again for a lovely night. It was such a fucking treat to get to go out to a fancy dinner while the rest of the poor suckers in the dorm were stuck in the common room, watching reruns of *Friends*. She felt like she had simultaneously achieved so many things: Marymount was grateful to her for keeping quiet about the whole embarrassing lockdown situation, so he was even more in her back pocket now; she'd had the most amazing time flirting with Julian—it was even kind of fun to flirt with stodgy old Brandon, who seemed to get a thrill out of it too; and she'd had the most delicious crème brulée in all of upstate New York. Not bad for last-minute plans.

The two boys were standing in the first-floor hallway, leaning on either side of the bathroom door, each holding a

Waverly mug, looking like very conscientious Owls. They looked kind of cute together—compact and tight (and uptight) Brandon, with his perfectly tousled hair gelled into place, wearing an Armani sweater over a button-down shirt, and gangly Julian, some sort of ratty ski cap on his head, his bleached-out dirty-blond hair poking out the bottom like straw. He was wearing a Question Authority T-shirt over a red thermal shirt and a pair of dark brown suit pants, clearly from a thrift store. They were sort of like the Odd Couple—or Starsky and Hutch, the Ben Stiller–Owen Wilson version.

She strutted down the hallway in their direction, her heels clicking against the polished marble floors. Both boys looked up at her. For as long as she could remember, Brandon seemed to despise her. Now he wore that same glassy-eyed look she was used to getting from guys who were into her. Although it was flattering, she knew he just wasn't her type. Brandon was wound a little too tight and probably was due for a stress-induced heart attack by age twenty-six.

As for Julian . . . she definitely seemed to be making progress on getting him to fall in love with her. And she was enjoying it, too. Maybe a little too much.

Tinsley's phone buzzed just as she waved hello to the guys. She flicked it open and saw a text from Heath saying TEACHER ALERT. *Shit.*

"Someone's coming—you guys had better hide." Tinsley ran down the rest of the hallway and pushed open the door to the bathroom and the boys dashed in behind her.

"Gee, thanks for looking out for us, Carmichael." Clearly Brandon wasn't ready to let all of his bitterness go—good. She liked to see him conflicted. It kept things interesting. Calling her by her last name was a blatant attempt to try and convince himself that he saw her as just one of the guys—ha. Fat chance.

Tinsley blew him a kiss. "Thought you'd like to see the inside of one of these places." The bathrooms in Dumbarton were surprisingly large and had been updated a few years ago. They were a little more modern than the rest of the building, with three toilet stalls tastefully done in a dark oak, a long wall with a mirror and three sinks, and three shower stalls around the corner.

"It's so neat in here," Julian remarked, his eyes running across the shelf of cubbies above the sinks where the girls stored their bath and shower things. She didn't tell him that things were definitely not usually this clean—but since they had nothing better to do today, the girls had made a point of straightening up their cubbies, wiping the crust off toothpaste tubes, removing stray tampons from view, and lining up their facial products in neat rows. "But wow. There's a whole lot of face shit in here." From one cubby, he picked up a bottle of Benefit Fantasy Mint Wash and another of L'Occitane's olive water face toner. "What's all this *for*?"

"One's a cleanser and the other's a toner." Brandon touched the L'Occitane bottle. "That's good stuff."

Tinsley giggled. Brandon certainly didn't help himself sometimes. She knew he was sensitive and all, but it was still sort of weird that Brandon knew more about skin care than she did. "That's mine. Put it back, please!"

Julian lifted the bottle out of her reach. "No way. I want to try out this magic potion." He twisted off the cap of the toner and poured some into his palm, then slapped it to his cheek and spread it around like aftershave. "Do I look different? Am I beautiful now?"

"No," Brandon replied at the same time Tinsley said, "Yes."

Brandon rolled his eyes. "You don't exactly have Tinsley's delicate skin, you know."

My delicate skin? It was Tinsley's turn to roll her eyes. Brandon trying to flirt with her sounded like Brandon sucking up to her, and that was definitely not a turn-on. He'd have better luck sticking with the sarcasm.

"What's this?" Julian peeked around the corner where the three shower stalls were tucked. The shower stalls were covered in beautiful cerulean blue Mediterranean-style tiles, donated by Sage Francis's family, who ran a ceramics company in western Massachusetts. They were fairly spotless, as the cleaning staff came in on Saturday mornings, apparently unaffected by the lockdown. He swept aside the white nylon curtain and let out a low whistle.

"Shit. Our showers were last renovated in like 1945. It's like a spa in here," Brandon commented jealously.

Julian stepped inside the first stall. "So this is where it all happens?" He had a goofy grin on his face, like he was channeling all the naked girls who showered in that exact spot every day.

Tinsley stepped in with him. "This is the one I always use."

He raised his eyebrows. "Oh, yeah? How come?"

Tinsley shrugged and perched her toe on the soap dish that was built into the wall. "It's handier for shaving legs."

"Damn." Julian shook his head. "You're right. That does make it handier. I wish we had one of those in our shower."

Tinsley giggled. She glanced up at his head, which almost hit the shower faucet. He was so freaking tall. "How come you're wearing a hat?" she asked.

He pretended to rub soap over his body. "It's actually a hot-oil treatment for my follicles—it just looks like a hat."

Something about Julian made Tinsley feel all goofy. As he dipped back his head, pretending to rinse his hair, Tinsley reached past him and turned on the faucet.

But he must have sensed what she was doing because just as her hand left the dial, he wrapped his arms around her waist and spun her around in front of him, ducking down and using her as a shield. She got a face full of cold water.

She shrieked and squirmed, but Julian's arms were wrapped tightly around her. The water was freezing! Finally she was able to reach out in front of her and slam the dial back in place.

"You ass!" She twirled back around to face him, her hair and body completely drenched.

The bathroom door slammed shut. Brandon must have left.

"Does the water always take that long to heat up?" Julian's lips twitched a little as he tried not to smile. "Maybe you should call a plumber." He stepped back and leaned against the tile wall, his gaze admiring.

Tinsley glowered at him, her carefully curled and volumized hair now lying in wet strings in front of her face, and her dress, Kara's dress, beautiful and sexy before, now felt like a soggy pink Kleenex clinging to her skin. Somehow Julian had managed to stay almost completely dry.

Not for long.

"You think that's funny?" Tinsley demanded, clenching her molars together to keep from laughing. "You think you're so smart?" Then she dove at him, throwing her soaked arms around his waist and pressing her wet face to his chest, rubbing back and forth to dry off her head. It was exciting, being this close to him—it was sort of like wrestling with a boy when you're a kid, and you get all excited but don't really know why.

Which, unfortunately, reminded her that Julian *was* kind of a kid still. He was a freshman, so he was, what? *Fourteen?* Maybe fifteen. Tinsley shivered, and this time it had nothing to do with the cold water. Jesus. A freshman. That meant he was taking Ancient and Medieval History of the World with Mr. DeWitt, the only class that had made Tinsley actually consider jabbing a pen in her eye socket just so that she could be excused. Freshmen on boys sports teams were forced to do silly things like wear pink underwear or garter belts under their uniforms; they had to have weekly meetings with their advisers to discuss academic "strategies for success," as Marymount had coined the term; in cafeteria lines, upperclassmen were practically allowed to skip ahead of them—or at least they did.

A WAVERLY OWL DOESN'T JUDGE SOMEONE BY THEIR SHOES

If the sight of Tinsley and Julian fawning all over each other hadn't been enough to make Brandon want to vomit, the sound of them having a water fight or wet T-shirt contest or whatever they hell they were doing definitely was. Brandon stormed out of the girls' bathroom, furious at himself for being, once again, a horrible judge of character. What was it about Tinsley that made everyone always so willing to accept her flaws? Just because she was beautiful? There were plenty of girls at Waverly who were prettier than Tinsley—okay, maybe not plenty. But a few. Or at least, Callie. But only Tinsley had such a devoted following. Freshman girls aspired to be her; even teachers, and not even just the ultra-slimy ones like Eric Dalton, seemed to be in awe of her. Why? Because of her freaky violet eyes that seemed to have some sort of x-ray vision into people's minds? Maybe she was a mutant. His comic book freak roommate certainly seemed to think she had some sort of sexual superpowers.

"Whoa!" Brandon cried, almost tripping over his own feet as he skidded to a stop. Standing in front of him was a pretty young woman in a black leather jacket and tight gray wool skirt that skimmed the tops of her tan leather Børn clogs. Her black cat's-eye glasses were perched sexily about halfway down her nose, and she looked through them at Brandon quizzically. *Shit.* "I was just, um, just . . ."

"Using the bathroom?" The girl's face curled into an amused grin. On closer inspection, it was clear that this was a teenage girl and not a teacher, as he'd first suspected. Her face was definitely too young, and she had a single silver hoop earring perched on the top of her right ear. Her features were strong: the kind of long nose and dramatic cheekbones that cameras love, and Brandon found himself wondering if she'd ever been in a Gucci eyewear ad because she looked vaguely familiar. "That's not a crime, you know."

"So . . ." Brandon tried to regain his composure. "I take it you're not a teacher?"

"Now you're catching on, Einstein." She tossed her head a little, and Brandon saw that the underside of her dirty-blond hair was a dark brown. She looked like the type who'd be in an all-girl band. Hot. The Børn clogs were not his thing (a little too granola), but on her they looked kind of punk rock hippie badass.

Or maybe he was being influenced by those dark brown eyes that had zeroed in on him. This was definitely not a Waverly Owl.

He cleared his throat. "So why are you here?"

The girl pursed her lips together. There was a small mole about an inch below the outside corner of her left eye. Insanely, Brandon couldn't tear his eyes away from it. It was like a magnet or something. "Looking for someone," she answered with a shrug. "You haven't, uh, seen Jeremiah Mortimer . . . have you?" A slow blush crept over her cheeks.

Interesting. Jeremiah didn't even go to this school and his fans were tracking him down here? Wait till Brett found out. Word was that Jeremiah was blowing off all the St. Lucius homecoming parties to sneak over to Dumbarton and hang out with her, and Brett was probably not looking forward to having to share him with anyone else.

Definitely not someone this hot.

"I hear he's around, but, um . . . I haven't seen him." Which was the truth. Normally Brandon would have been bummed that she was asking about another guy, but he was still pretty sure she was flirting with him. He leaned against the peach-colored wall and gazed up at a water stain on the peeling plaster ceiling. A giggle escaped from the bathroom, but Brandon ignored it. "You go to St. Lucius?"

The girl nodded and glanced down the empty hallway. She tapped her long, unpainted fingernails against the dark wood molding around the bathroom door. "Are all your parties this, um, wild and crazy?"

"Nah, sometimes they're boring." Brandon smiled with closed lips and ran his tongue over his teeth, just in case she hadn't actually been flirting with him but instead had been transfixed by a piece of spinach in his teeth. When he was sure it was safe, he smiled. "I'm Brandon, by the way."

Her dark eyes returned his inviting stare. "I'm Elizabeth."

"My dog's name is Elizabeth!" Brandon blurted before realizing that maybe it wasn't the smoothest thing to say. But it just came out, and he did miss his family's Labrador—she was just about the only thing that made going back home to Westport for Christmas and vacations even remotely bearable. He certainly wasn't going to say it, but now that he thought of it, Elizabeth the girl's liquidy brown eyes *did* kind of remind him of Elizabeth the dog's. In a good way, of course.

God, he was a tool.

"No kidding?" Elizabeth actually laughed—a sweet melodic sound that reminded Brandon of the way the first few notes seemed to burst to life off the strings of his violin. *Cut the poetry, Brandon. Concentrate. Don't make any more stupid remarks while trying to flirt.* "It's not, like, a poodle or a bichon or anything, is it? I don't want any of those prissy dogs giving my name a bad rap."

"She's a shepherd-Lab mix, and she looks pretty tough when she's tearing apart the Sunday *Times*." Brandon watched in awe as Elizabeth slid a wisp of dirty-blond hair behind her ear and pushed her glasses back into place, all in one smooth motion. There was something so sexy about girls who could wear glasses with confidence. "Not prissy at all. In fact, I once saw her kick the shit out of our neighbor's Rhodesian ridgeback."

Elizabeth pretended to think about it, scratching the nape of her neck with her right hand. Her jacket sleeve slid up to reveal one of those braided cotton sailor's bracelets, the kind you find in just about every souvenir store on Cape Cod, on the verge of disintegration. "I guess that's all right." She shifted her weight from one foot to the other and toyed with the zipper on her jacket. "So what do you say we get this party started?"

Brandon stared at the zipper for a second, thinking, maybe she was talking about . . . taking off her clothes? What kind of crazy girl *was* she? He almost stopped breathing.

But then she caught him staring and poked his stomach with her index finger. "I didn't mean *that*, you dirty boy." Her eyes sparkled. "I meant, let's go wake everyone up." Immediately she stalked over to the closest dorm room, winked at Brandon, and gave it a sharp knock.

After a minute, a timid-looking blond girl opened the door and peeked out.

"Did you know that there's a party going on out here?" Elizabeth demanded, her voice stern and full of authority. Brandon watched her profile from afar.

"Uh—uh, no!" the girl stuttered, even though it was clear she was wearing party clothes—a red pleat-front miniskirt (was that Callie's Diane von Furstenberg?) and black tank top that said FREE WINONA in rhinestones (definitely not Callie's). "I didn't know about any party."

Elizabeth placed both hands on her slim hips. "Well, why the hell not?" She burst into laughter, and Brandon couldn't help joining in. She had so much *energy*. The girl in the Winona shirt stared at both of them before clutching a hand to her heart.

"Oh my God, you gave me a fucking *heart* attack." She quickly dashed into her room and reappeared waggling her empty Waverly mug. "I ran out of beer, like, ten minutes ago, and I've been dying in here."

Feeling completely relaxed in a way he'd never felt before, Brandon led the way down the hall, pounding on all the doors, scaring the kids hiding inside before dragging them out to the party again. He and Elizabeth raced up to the second floor. As his Adidas sneakers slammed against the marbles steps and he glanced over at the amazingly funky girl clomping up the stairs in her crunchy clogs beside him, he wondered where the hell she'd been his whole life.

A WAVERLY OWL KNOWS THAT WHERE THERE'S INCENSE, THERE'S FIRE.

Once Tinsley left the room, Brett and Jeremiah didn't take long to make up for lost time. She'd been craving him all day, like the peanut butter M&M cookies dining services made every other Monday. It was kind of nice having him all to herself instead of sharing him with the adoring St. Lucius masses. And she couldn't help thinking how totally sweet it was that he would rather sneak away and be with her than stick around and get drunk at the countless victory parties that had to be going on all over his campus. Practically in his honor, since he was the one who'd won the game.

But he was here. In Brett's bed. Wearing his Gap boxers with the bulldogs on them and nothing else. Iron & Wine, Brett's favorite mood music, was playing, and she'd lit a couple of cones of sandalwood incense.

"Does it hurt here?" she asked, placing her hand on his shoulder. The two of them were lying face-to-face under her thick down comforter, Brett's head propped up on Jeremiah's left arm. Brett felt a little shy in her black strapless Le Mystère bra and matching low-rise briefs. But it wasn't like Jeremiah hadn't seen her body before, and besides, it was really like she was just wearing a bikini. But things felt different now—now that she thought she was ready for more.

Jeremiah tried not to grimace. "It hurts everywhere, babe."

"Here?" She slowly slid her hand down his chest, over the GET GOOSED paint.

"Actually, that makes it feel a little better." Jeremiah cleared his throat, and his eyes had that dreamy expression they got when he was completely turned on, which Brett loved. It made her feel like the most attractive girl on the planet and so powerful. She hoped that didn't mean she was destined to become a dominatrix one day.

But when Jeremiah leaned over and kissed her, all of Brett's thoughts disappeared. She'd never felt so comfortable before, so relaxed. So ready. "How many times did you get tackled today?"

Jeremiah traced his big fingers clumsily over the gold hoop earrings high up on Brett's left earlobe. He groaned. "About fifty."

Boldly she grabbed the waistband of his boxers and pulled him closer. "Fifty-one," she murmured in his ear. "You locked the door, right?"

"I think so," he said back, kissing her neck. His hand slid down to the small of her back. He was practically panting.

"There's . . . um . . . something I wanted to tell you." Brett was finding it incredibly hard to think of anything besides how delicious Jeremiah's lips felt on her skin. She felt like she was drunk, but she hadn't even taken a sip of beer.

"Okay." Jeremiah kept nibbling on her shoulder. She had to push him away in order to come up with even one coherent thought.

And this was important.

"You know how I told you, a long time ago, about how I . . . uh . . . slept with that Swiss guy? And that was my first time?"

"How could I forget?" Jeremiah rested his head on her pillow and stared into her eyes. He played with the gold starfish pendant hanging around her neck. It looked so tiny compared to his huge hands.

"Well, that wasn't exactly true." She took a big gulp.

"Oh." Jeremiah stopped playing with the pendant and let it fall back against Brett's bare skin. "Well . . . um . . . it's okay if, you know, you've been with someone else too. It doesn't really matter what you did before me. I'm okay with it." He kissed the tip of her nose tenderly.

"That's . . . that's not what I meant." She could hear people running around in the hallways. What was going on out there? "Nothing really happened with that guy. Or with any other guy."

"You mean . . ."

"When you told me you were a virgin, I should have told you the truth. That I am too." She wrinkled her nose. "I'm sorry I wasn't honest about it."

Jeremiah was quiet for a few seconds, and at first Brett thought maybe he was pissed. But then he touched her chin and smiled, his row of crooked bottom teeth looking extra cute. "I don't care. It's just about me and you, right?"

"Yes!" Brett breathed a huge sigh of relief, amazed at how nervous she'd been. Of course Jeremiah understood. He always did. A flood of emotions rushed through her, almost causing her eyes to tear up, but she blinked them back. She really . . . *loved* him, didn't she? Everything just seemed so right. So perfect.

"You're just so beautiful, you know?" he whispered, and ran his hand up and down Brett's arm, sending tingles all the way down to her toes. She felt like she did in the seconds right before making a field hockey shot, when adrenaline coursed through her veins, heightening all her senses and making her super-aware of how the grass felt beneath her spikes, how blue the sky was, how her teammates were screaming from the sidelines. Her heart was practically in her mouth.

"I think . . ." She grabbed his hand and pressed it to her heart. Silly, but she wanted him to feel how it was pounding. "I think I'm ready now. Like, really ready."

At that exact moment, there was a loud, sharp knock on the door. "Open up!" a woman's voice cried. Brett's heart almost pounded right out of her chest. She and Jeremiah jumped apart. "Under the bed!" she hissed. "Or no—the closet!"

Jeremiah dove toward the closet, snagging his toe on Brett's throw rug and crashing loudly into Tinsley's desk chair, sending it sprawling across the hardwood floor. "Fuck!" he shouted, his loud Boston accent ringing through the room and probably out into the hallway.

The door flew open, and Brett wanted to die. This was the end, wasn't it? She was going to be *expelled*. But then someone said, "Jeremiah?" A girl Brett had never seen before stood in the doorway, looking startled.

Uh, hello? She was surprised? What about Brett, almost naked under her covers and on the verge of the most important moment in her life, only to be interrupted by this blond chick in über-trendy glasses who seemed to know *her* boyfriend? What was going on?

"Elizabeth! Uh . . . what are you doing here?" Jeremiah picked up the chair and rubbed his left knee.

Elizabeth?

The girl glanced at Brett for a moment like she was sizing her up. Brett, her covers pulled up to her neck, stared back at her defiantly. This was her room, damn it, and she wasn't going to let some St. Lucius football groupie chase down Jeremiah and then examine her like she was some specimen in a petri dish. The girl turned back to Jeremiah, clearly flustered—or upset?—at seeing him half naked. "Brandon and I . . . were just, um . . . getting the party started again."

For the first time, Brett noticed that Brandon Buchanan was standing next to the girl, his cheeks flushed red. At least he had the courtesy to be embarrassed about barging in on some people who were clearly enjoying their privacy.

"Hey, Brett." Brandon adjusted the collar of his polo shirt. Brett glared back at him.

"Well, um . . . Brett and I were just on our way out there," Jeremiah mumbled. Right, on their way to a party sans clothing?

He glanced at Brett and shrugged apologetically, and she felt like tearing out her hair at the unfairness of it all. "This is . . . uh . . ." (*Don't you dare forget my name,* Brett cursed) "Brett. Brett . . . this is . . . my friend Elizabeth."

The two girls eyed each other uneasily. Maybe it was just because Jeremiah was so clearly flustered too, but everything seemed so totally suspicious, and Brett wasn't even the insanely jealous type, like Callie. Brett smiled weakly at the girl, who smiled weakly back at her. Why was she even *here* if she went to St. Lucius? Didn't she have homecoming parties to go to? And who the hell was this *friend* to look so uncomfortable after seeing Jeremiah in bed with his girlfriend? Or to barge into Brett's room like that?

And why was her hair two colors, like a skunk?

Brandon spoke up first. "We should probably get out of here. Let you guys get . . . uh . . . ready." He placed a hand on Elizabeth's arm, almost protectively. How did *he* know her so well?

"Oh. Yeah," Elizabeth mumbled in a spaced-out voice. "We'll see you out there."

"Yeah. See ya." Jeremiah picked up his shirt from the floor as the two of them disappeared out into the hallway.

Brett didn't know what to think. Or what to *feel*. She threw off her heavy comforter, feeling suddenly hot. The gorgeous dress she'd borrowed from Rifat was lying in a green puddle on the floor, and she just wasn't in the mood to put it on again. "That was weird," she said to Jeremiah, watching his face for a reaction.

He finished buttoning up his shirt and stood next to her. "I'm sorry we were interrupted." He touched her hair. "But there'll be other chances." He grabbed his jeans from the floor.

Other chances? Sure, the mood was totally shattered, but shouldn't Jeremiah be dying to re-create it? It was still early—why didn't he want to, you know, try again? Brett certainly wasn't in the mood now, but still . . . it would have been nice if he tried. She could hear music start up down the hall.

Bitterly she pulled a pair of wide-legged dark denim jeans from her closet and stepped into them. As she searched through her closet for a shirt, she glanced over her shoulder at Jeremiah, who was staring at her. "What?" she asked, somewhat crankily. She tugged a sleeveless black turtleneck from its hanger.

Jeremiah shook his head. "Nothing. You just look really sexy, standing there in your bra." *Brah.* His Boston accent brought a smile to Brett's lips for the first time since their interruption.

But still. As she pulled her shirt over her head, she couldn't help wondering what he wasn't saying.

A WAVERLY OWL IS SMART ENOUGH NOT TO KISS AND TELL.

As Easy sat in the bottom of Callie's closet, enjoying the familiar taste of her kiss—the combination of smoky cloves and vanilla-y lipstick and . . . was that pot? Callie always hated it when Easy smoked weed, a fairly common occurrence since he shared a room with Alan St. Girard, whose hippie parents grew the stuff. She'd tell him he smelled like a Dave Matthews concert and would refuse to kiss him, but Easy knew she was mostly pissed off by the way smoking made him turn in on himself and away from her. She was always asking him what he was thinking, like she couldn't stand that there was a place she didn't have access to. It drove him a little crazy.

So what the hell was he doing here, with his tongue in her mouth? *Jenny,* he thought. She was supposed to be coming back with beer. What if she came in right now? His stomach dropped, like he was on a roller coaster going down a huge hill and he suddenly realized his safety harness thingy wasn't latched.

Easy pulled away, his mind reeling. Something frilly tickled his ear.

In the darkness, Callie whispered, "What are you thinking?"

"I think we should get out of here," Easy mumbled. He fumbled for the doorknob in the dark, finally finding it and pushing. Light flooded in. Callie was crouched next to him, looking as confused as he felt. "We should . . . probably get downstairs. People are going to wonder."

"Yeah. Otherwise it'll look suspicious." She stood up first, untangling her long, thin body. Her short pigtails bounced as she moved. "Why don't you go first? I've gotta find shoes, anyway."

Easy took a long, deep breath before standing up. "Okay. See you later," and closed the room door behind him. Each step he took down the stairs seemed to say *asshole, asshole, asshole.* Had he really just made out with Callie? The last few months of their relationship, even when they'd been apart, had been fairly excruciating. She was always nagging him until he felt like exploding. He tried to conjure up specific instances, but for some reason, he couldn't. He could only picture her laughing at dinner with his dad or defending his artwork. Or sliding down next to him in the dark closet.

What was wrong with him? Had he really made a mistake by breaking up with her, or was he just seeing Callie through rose-colored glasses now? Was he destined to be one of those assholes who only wanted the girls he couldn't have?

Fuck. And then there was Jenny. He needed to talk to Jenny, but he couldn't even make sense of what he was feeling, so how was he supposed to be able to say something about it? He didn't want to hurt her . . . and he didn't want to lose her, either.

Was that so wrong, to be in love with two girls at the same time? Was it even possible?

"Hey!" Jenny was coming out of one of the dorm rooms, a Waverly mug in each hand. Her face lit up when she saw him. "I'm sorry I took so long—there was some kind of false alarm and we were all hiding."

Hiding. Right. Like in dark closets. "It's okay." He took a mug from her hand. "Thanks." He sipped it. "Mmm, warm beer." Served him right—that's about all he deserved at the moment.

Jenny was so trusting—if he'd been upstairs, supposedly alone, for ten minutes, Callie would want to know what he'd been doing. But it didn't seem to cross Jenny's mind that he would have been doing anything suspicious, which made him feel like a total slimebag.

"Could you guys untangle yourselves for, like, three seconds and come play I Never?" Heath Ferro demanded, looking mentally unbalanced wearing a girl's tank top that said FREE WINONA in sparkles. The shirt was ten sizes too small for him, which he probably thought was perfect as it gave him a chance to show off the six-pack abs he was always bragging about.

"Only if you put on a shirt first, dude." Easy shook his head. "I'm not sure how long I can look at that."

"What happened to the one you were wearing, Heath?" Jenny asked innocently.

Heath smirked. "You mean this one's not making an *impression* on you?"

Jenny glanced from one to the other, an uncomprehending look on her face. Easy wanted to pound Heath to the floor but decided to take the high road instead. "Fine. We're coming."

"I wish we could play a different game," Jenny said, heading toward the common room. Easy found himself sliding his arm around her shoulders. It just seemed to go there. "Whatever happened to Trivial Pursuit?" she joked.

"Nerd," Easy said softly, kissing the top of her head. He just wanted to make everything right again—with Jenny and with Callie. How the hell was he supposed to do that when he wanted to kiss them both?

The Twister game in the corner had turned up a notch, with Ryan Reynolds and Alan St. Girard involved, pretzeling up with the girls still playing. Benny Cunningham was on one of the couches next to Lon Baruzza, who was twirling one of her long ponytails around his wrist as she giggled and touched his knee.

"Glad you kids could join us." Tinsley's smile curled into its inevitable smirk. Tinsley was in a white T-shirt and a brown miniskirt with suspenders—no one wore suspenders, ever, and so of course she looked unbearably cool. Or not. She looked kind of like Roller Girl from *Boogie Nights*—enough to drive the boys insane. She sat on the arm of a leather couch, her shoes balanced on the coffee table, looking mellower than she had at the Ritz-Bradley party. Good. Maybe that meant she'd be keeping her clothes on, although by the way Julian was practically hanging off her, it looked like he was hoping for an impromptu striptease.

"Everyone got a full mug?" Brandon Buchanan asked. He was sitting in a fat armchair with an unbelievably pretty girl with black-and-blond hair in an unzipped leather jacket and a blue T-shirt that said FREE TIBET, a funny contrast to the Winona shirt. Brandon's hair was all messed up, and in a way that looked unintentional. The girl kept glancing nervously in the direction of Jeremiah and Brett. Brett sat on the floor with a pissy look on her face while Jeremiah sat behind her on the couch and played with her hair. A quiet girl in Easy's math class—Tara? Kara?—was sitting on the couch between Jeremiah and a small, bird-like blond girl wearing a black minidress that looked like something Tinsley would wear. Wasn't that the weird saxophone player? Where had all these chicks come from? Math class girl waved at Jenny.

"That's Kara," Jenny whispered into Easy's ear. "She's really cool."

Callie appeared, seemingly out of nowhere, looking a little flustered. She purposely didn't look in Easy and Jenny's direction as she slid onto the couch next to Benny.

"Where've you been?" Tinsley demanded, staring at Callie's face. Callie just shrugged.

"Regular rules this time," Jenny spoke up, glancing at Heath, who liked to add rules like you had to make out with him no matter what. "If you've done it, you have to drink."

"I'll start," Heath Ferro exclaimed, taking a last good-luck chug from his mug. "I've never . . . made out in the horse stables."

Jackass, Easy thought. Heath was clearly trying to embarrass Easy, and Callie, and Jenny. Why did he have to be such a prick? Thankfully, Easy wasn't the only one who found the stables romantic—along with himself and Callie and Jenny, Lon Baruzza and the skinny blond girl took swigs of their beer too. Neither Jenny nor Callie even glanced in Easy's direction.

"Surprised you haven't been there, Pony," Benny Cunningham teased Heath. "You've been everywhere else."

"I don't get off on the smell of horse shit, I guess," Heath grumbled.

"I'll go," Jenny said. Everyone's eyes turned to her, and Easy couldn't help thinking how completely adorable she looked with her hair pulled back like that. "I've never had someone throw a beer in my face. Tonight."

Everyone seemed kind of puzzled until Heath lifted his mug and took a giant slurp and everyone burst out laughing. Easy would have liked to have been there for that.

"So that explains the outfit, at least." Tinsley laughed. "Who did it?"

"You don't get to ask questions in this game, Carmichael. Stick to the rules." Heath glowered into his beer.

"I'll go next," the bird girl spoke up eagerly after the laughter subsided. "Um . . . I've never had sex before."

Holy shit. Way to ignore the subtleties of the game and drop the bomb right away. That was one of those questions that people always kind of hinted at, not really wanting to ask.

The room seemed to fall silent as everyone stared at each other, daring someone to move first.

"Duh!" Heath said, raising his mug to his lips and taking another giant swig. Lon Baruzza followed, with Benny smiling at him appreciatively as she took a sip too. Tinsley rocked back with a laugh. Guess Benny C. wasn't as prudish as she liked to pretend. Then, almost at the same moment, Jeremiah and leather jacket girl met each other's eyes across the room and raised their mugs quickly, as if hoping no one would notice. But both their faces were completely red, and Tinsley, along with everyone else, immediately assumed they had done it with each other. No one moved. Tinsley looked at Brett, who kept her head down as she fiddled with the strap of her shoe.

"Back up a minute." Heath raised his hands and tried to make noise like a truck backing up. "Tinsley Carmichael, Miss I've Been Everywhere and Done Everything, are you trying to say that you are as pure and untouched as virgin snow?"

"Why is that so surprising, Heath? Just because I wouldn't sleep with you?" Tinsley shot back at him, her cheeks red.

Heath pretended to pull an arrow out of his heart.

"You've got to be kidding me." Callie glanced from Brett to Tinsley, looking more than pissed, holding her palms up in "what the fuck" manner. "You guys are *both* virgins? What happened to being honest with your roommates?"

Tinsley rolled her eyes exaggeratedly, as if she couldn't believe what a big deal everyone was turning this into.

"I could think of half a dozen times you've implied that you were less than *virginal*," Callie pointed out, focusing on

Tinsley, all riled up now for some reason. She hated being lied to, even about something that wasn't really any of her business. "What about Mr. Dalton? Chiedo from South Africa?"

A bunch of other girls jumped in to point out all the other times Tinsley hadn't exactly told the truth. Easy couldn't really give a shit about Tinsley, though—and he wasn't exactly surprised. She'd lie about anything if it was to her benefit and he'd never believed a word out of her mouth. But he did watch Brett with interest. She'd always implied that she wasn't exactly innocent, but he'd thought her tough attitude was a maybe just a cover-up for some kind of complex.

Although now Brett wasn't coming up with anything. Her hands were shaking as Jeremiah whispered frantically in her ear and tried to calm her down. Apparently Jeremiah's revelation had come as a surprise to her too. And what was the deal between him and FREE TIBET?

Tinsley's irritation had reached its peak. She stood up abruptly and practically shouted at Callie, "I never said I had *sex*, okay? Get over it."

That pissed Easy off. "What about . . ." he started to ask, thinking of the time Tinsley had spent the night at some Columbia grad student's apartment and bragged about it all over campus the next day.

"What about we play the game?" Tinsley fiddled with her suspenders and straightened her skirt. "I'll go," she said quickly, before anyone could say anything else. "*I* never took my *ex*-girlfriend out to dinner with my dad instead of my *current* girlfriend."

Easy's stomach dropped. Everyone glanced around, totally confused and thinking that maybe stress had caused Tinsley to actually go insane. She was staring straight at Easy, her violet eyes flashing with anger. What did she have to be angry about, that bitch? He glared back at her.

"Why aren't you drinking, Easy?" she asked nastily. "You know the rules."

If she weren't a girl, he would have thrown his drink in her face at that moment. But it wouldn't have mattered—she'd already accomplished what she'd intended. Namely, her scandal was no longer in the spotlight, and his was.

Heath chuckled, a deep "Ho ho ho," like it was the funniest thing in the world.

Jenny's face slowly drained of color. She stood up to face him. "Is that . . . is that true?"

Easy could feel everyone watching him, and not all of their looks were kind. Not that he cared right now what anyone else thought. He just wanted to stop Jenny from hating him. "Well . . . uh . . . not really . . . but sort of . . ." Not his most eloquent response, but it didn't really matter as Jenny quickly backed away and ran out of the room.

The room buzzed with noise, and Easy pressed his hands to his head as if he could have any hope of blocking it out. Kara, the girl Jenny had waved to, jumped up from her seat and ran out after Jenny, not too fast to avoid giving Easy a nasty look on her way out. Brett stood up and rushed out of the room, with Jeremiah chasing after her.

Looked like the party was over.

Callie stood up, her voice brimming with fury. "Why would you do that?" she demanded, walking over to Tinsley and standing directly in front of her.

"Well . . . you can all talk about my secrets. Why shouldn't everyone know about *his*?" She shot Easy a glare.

Callie shook her head, her little blond pigtails flapping. "You are a total bitch."

Tinsley seemed at a loss for words for the first time in her life. Her mouth trembled a little, not like she was going to cry, but like she was trying to narrow in on the absolute perfect scathing comeback. But after a few seconds, she just tossed her hair and stalked out of the room.

About fucking time, Easy thought. Too bad she couldn't keep her mouth shut for the rest of her life.

A WAVERLY OWL KNOWS THAT A SUCCESSFUL RELATIONSHIP IS BUILT ON HONESTY.

After storming out of the party, the last place Brett wanted to be was her bedroom, where, an hour ago, she'd been on the verge of having sex for the very first time with the boyfriend she loved. She'd thought everything was perfect—but now it was clear that it had all been fake. She and Jeremiah couldn't make the grand, symbolic gesture of giving their virginity to each other because he'd already lost it—to that *other* girl. And it wasn't like it was something that had happened a long time ago. No, when she and Jeremiah were dating before, he was definitely a virgin. They break up, get back together two weeks later, and suddenly he's not a virgin anymore? What the fuck? The thought of going back to her room, to her Iron & Wine and her sandalwood incense and her drawn shades, made her ill. Not like stomping up the stairs to the roof was any better—she still felt ill. What she really wanted to do was run out the front door of Dumbarton, hop in a car, and drive somewhere fast, but she couldn't leave Dumbarton, so the roof was as far away as she could get.

She flung open the metal door and stepped out into the dark, cool night air. Her arms were immediately covered with goose bumps, but she didn't notice. It was a beautiful night, which just pissed Brett off even more. Each one of the ten billion stars in the sky seemed to be shining happily down on her, and she wanted to kill all of them.

The door flew open. Jeremiah, practically panting, stepped toward her, but Brett backed away. She hoped his body was in even more pain now after running up three flights of stairs. "How could you? How could you . . . do that . . . and not say anything to me?" she shouted, not caring who heard.

"Brett, please. Calm down, okay?"

"I told you I was a *virgin*. I told you I was ready to do it. Were you *ever* going to tell me the truth?"

"Yes! Of course." Jeremiah shoved his hands into the pockets of his dark jeans, his face looking like his dog had just died. *Good,* Brett thought meanly. *He deserves to feel bad.* "It just wasn't . . . the right time."

"So when would be the right time?" Brett couldn't keep the venom out of her voice. She just felt so betrayed. Jeremiah was supposed to be one of the *good guys*. He was one of the anti–Eric Daltons, the kind of guy who *doesn't* sleep around or ditch you for the next hot thing that walks into the room. He wasn't supposed to do this to her. "After we'd done it? Because if Brandon and . . ." Brett could not bring herself to say

Elizabeth's name. "If Brandon and *Bitchface* hadn't interrupted when they did . . ."

"I would have told you," Jeremiah insisted, pulling a Camel Light from a crushed package and sticking it between his lips. He fumbled in his pockets for a lighter. "But you know, you were lying to me for months. Why'd you lie about being a virgin?"

"Because . . . because . . ." Brett sputtered. "I don't know. It was none of anyone else's business." And what difference would it have made, anyway? If he'd known she was virgin, did that mean he wouldn't have jumped on Bitchface?

"None of anyone's business," Jeremiah repeated, inhaling deeply from his cigarette. "So why are you so pissed now if virginity is none of anyone else's business?"

"Don't twist my words around!" Brett felt so . . . helpless. She had never been so furious before, and she was angry at everything. Jeremiah. Herself. Elizabeth. She could have strangled her. All her thoughts were a complete jumble, churning through her brain at breakneck speed.

"We weren't even together when it happened," Jeremiah pointed out quietly. "It's not like *I* was the one who cheated. . . ."

"What?" That was so unfair of him to remind her of Mr. Dalton. She'd already apologized a million times for that. "I never slept with Eric."

"How was I supposed to know that?" Jeremiah suddenly looked more angry than sad. His floppy red hair fluttered in the wind. "You dump me—in a *voice mail*—with no explanation, you don't answer my calls or emails or texts, and then two days later I hear you're spending the night at this skeezy older guy's house. What was I supposed to think?"

Brett hated hearing about how she'd acted. It was pretty awful. "I know—I *know* I was a shitty person about it. How many times can I apologize?" Apparently not enough. "But did you have to go out and *sleep with* someone else? Jesus, Jeremiah." A hot tear slid down Brett's cheek, and she swiped at it angrily with the back of her hand. She turned away from him and walked over to the stone wall at the edge of the roof. The campus was quiet—patchworks of lights in the other dorms shone through the trees, and somewhere, at the other end of campus, the trustees were getting drunk off Dean Marymount's wine and having a grand old time. She rubbed her hands up and down her arms to keep warm.

She heard Jeremiah clear his throat. "You broke my heart, Brett." It sounded like he was going to cry, but then he took a puff of his cigarette and his voice steadied. "I was completely crushed. I didn't get it—I thought, you know, that you loved me."

"I did love you!" she cried. As soon as she said it, she realized how funny it felt to hear herself say it in the past tense—*loved*. As in, *loved once*, but not now. Two enormous owls took off from one of the huge oak trees and chased each other around campus. Brett wondered if the male owl ever messed around with other female owls and if the female owl was able to forgive him.

"Well, you had a fucking funny way of showing it."

"Don't you dare blame this on me." Brett whirled around to face him again. "You're the one who was clearly dying to get with someone else. How long did you wait? Like, a day? Two?"

Jeremiah flung his half-smoked cigarette down and ground it out with the toe of his booger green Pumas. Brett had always hated those shoes. "I had to talk about it—to people, to help me understand it. Elizabeth was a friend. She was there for me. And it just . . . happened. I wasn't thinking—I was too crushed to think anything."

Brett kicked at a piece of gravel with her toe, and it skidded across the roof. "I wanted you to be my first. That's why I couldn't sleep with Eric—it just wasn't right. I wanted it to be you." Clearly he hadn't felt that strongly about her if he could go and have sex with the first girl who tried to make him feel better. She'd waited seventeen years to lose her virginity—not that she'd been thinking about it for the first thirteen or fourteen. And when she finally figured out who it was that she loved, who she wanted to share it with . . . he'd already gone and done it with *Elizabeth*. Didn't that girl know any *other* ways to cheer a guy up? She suddenly remembered what it was like to play musical chairs and the music stopped and you were the one left standing like an idiot. It's what this felt like, times a billion.

"You gotta understand," Jeremiah pleaded. "You've never been heartbroken."

Brett swallowed the lump in her throat. "I have now."

"Brett . . ."

"So what was it like?" Brett couldn't help picturing Elizabeth and Jeremiah, naked, rolling around on his bed. Kissing. She wondered where they'd done it—his room? Hers? Out in a field? A cheap motel? What had Elizabeth been wearing? Did he tell her how beautiful she looked? Did he call her babe? "Was it good?"

Jeremiah didn't say anything for a long time. He just stared at her with his big blue-green eyes. "It wasn't you."

"We've been back together for over two weeks now," Brett said quietly, staring at the toe of her cream-colored moccasin. There was a black spot from where she'd kicked the gravel. "There wasn't a right time anywhere in there?"

"I didn't want you to break up with me. Again."

Brett stared at the stars, wishing they would just crash down on her right now and end it all. It was like she was being punished for so stupidly falling for Eric Dalton. Or even more than that, like she was being punished for lying about not being a virgin. Maybe if Jeremiah had known the truth about that, he wouldn't have been so quick to jump into Elizabeth's bed. A pessimistic little Dorothy Parker poem popped into her head:

By the time you swear you're his,
Shivering and sighing,
And he vows his passion is
Infinite, undying,
Lady, make a note of this—
One of you is lying.

It was true—they'd both lied to each other, and now they were in this ugly mess of their own creation. She felt all clammy, like she had the flu, and her knees were all wobbly. It was true that Jeremiah had been understanding enough to forgive her about her own indiscretion with Dalton. She had thought that meant he loved her. But if he loved her, how could he have slept with someone else? Brett took a deep breath.

"I think you should leave."

Instant Message Inbox

YvonneStidder: Yikes, was it my sex question that killed the party?

KaraWhalen: Sort of, but it's not your fault everyone lies about everything.

YvonneStidder: Right. Who would've thought T's never done it? It gives me hope. . . .

KaraWhalen: Honey, if you want to lose it, all you have to do is ask. Guys here are all horndogs.

YvonneStidder: Heath Ferro did look pretty cute tonight in his girl shirt.

KaraWhalen: You could do better than him if you closed your eyes and pulled a name out of the phone book.

YvonneStidder: You threw the beer at him, didn't you??

KaraWhalen: Guilty as charged.

A RESPONSIBLE OWL STANDS UP FOR HERSELF—EVEN IN THE FACE OF A VERY HOT GUY.

Callie wandered around the empty Dumbarton common room in a daze, still not quite believing what had just happened. She'd always known party games were dangerous—that's what made them fun—but usually dangerous meant she tended to do stupid things, like get drunk and make out with Heath Ferro. This time, it was sort of worse. She felt really, really bad—and for once, not for herself. For Jenny. It was kind of strange to suddenly feel sorry for the girl she'd been resenting for so long, but Jenny was nice. Jenny hadn't mentioned the fact that all of her hair bands had mysteriously disappeared, even though she must have noticed. Or the fact that Easy's sweet little drawing had also vanished. If their situations had been reversed, Callie would have certainly bitched about it. But Jenny was too nice to do anything.

She was still sort of a kid and so clearly in love with Easy

Walsh. Who, right now, was the only other person in the room, collapsed on the couch, nursing the beer he had just poured half a bottle of Jack Daniels into.

Callie stopped and surveyed the room. It definitely looked like there had just been a party here. And it smelled like it too. Waverly mugs and abandoned plastic cups partly filled with beer were scattered around the room. Great. All Pardee had to do was walk in early, she'd shit a brick, and the Dumbarton girls would probably be locked down for another month. Where had everyone gone? Just because Tinsley had to ruin the party didn't mean they didn't have to clean up after themselves. She wrinkled her nose and picked up a plastic cup. "The least you can do, you know, is help me out?"

Easy could barely lift his eyes in her direction. "Huh?"

"Would you stop thinking about yourself for, like, five minutes?" Callie disappeared down the hall into the kitchenette, which consisted of a refrigerator, crammed with leftover Chinese takeout cartons and moldy pizza, a sink, and a microwave that always burned everyone's popcorn. She poured the beer down the sink and rinsed out the cup before tossing it in the recycling bin. When she came back into the living room, Easy hadn't moved, which made her furious.

"What?" he said, noticing her glare. "What do you want me to do?"

She picked up two mugs off the coffee table and shoved Easy's feet onto the floor. "You can stop feeling sorry for yourself and start thinking about the other people involved."

"Maybe I already am."

"Maybe," Callie countered, stacking the mugs on top of each other and staring down at Easy, still loafing. "But you really should have been thinking about them before, when it *mattered*. It was really insensitive, what you did."

Easy groaned and rubbed his eyes with his fists, his drink teetering on his knee. "I *know*. I feel like a total jerk about it. . . ."

Callie could tell it was true that Easy felt horrible, but what about her? And what about Jenny? *Easy* was the one holding all the cards. It was *him* they both wanted, and he had abused that. "Well, good. 'Cause you've *been* a total jerk about it."

Easy didn't say anything, like he knew she was right. And Callie knew she was too. Suddenly it felt good to stand up to him. He couldn't just sit there and wallow in his own half-drunken stupor, feeling sorry for himself and wishing he were living in Paris already and didn't have to deal with all these crazy chicks. No, Easy needed to accept responsibility for the mess he had made.

Callie made another trip to the kitchen sink and dropped off the mugs, then picked up a crushed pizza box on her way back into the living room. A few half-eaten crusts rolled around inside. "Look, Easy. I don't mean to sound harsh, but it's unfair of you to think you can have things both ways. If you have feelings for Jenny, you can't have feelings for me anymore."

Which would be kind of sad . . . But still. Callie meant it. She didn't want to be *one* of Easy's girlfriends—she was either The One or nothing at all. No matter how great it had been to kiss him again—and it had been pretty freaking great—no guy was worth making a fool of herself over.

Easy stood up. "But it's not working that way."

"Well, it kind of has to. You need to figure out what you want." Callie stuffed some crinkled-up greasy napkins (gross!) into the pizza box and stood up, feeling somehow proud of herself. "And until you do, I kind of doubt either of us will want anything to do with you."

Instant Message Inbox

AlanStGirard: You hear what happened in the living room?

AlisonQuentin: What, that T and Brett are virgins? That Kara threw beer in HF's face? That Easy's fucking around on J with C?

AlanStGirard: Uh, yeah . . . how'd you know all that already?

AlisonQuentin: Baby, news travels fast when we've been locked up all day.

AlanStGirard: Feeling antsy? Wanna run around naked in the tunnels?

AlisonQuentin: Not a chance. Haven't you realized that secrets don't stay secrets here?

AlanStGirard: What about in your room? Do secrets stay secret there??? ;)

AlisonQuentin: A responsible Owl never invites boys to her room . . . (but she doesn't turn them away, either!)

A WAVERLY OWL IS NOT AFRAID OF THE DARK—AND SOMETIMES EMBRACES IT.

"That was a bit of a disaster, don't you think?" Elizabeth said lightly as she leaned with Brandon against the basement stairwell banister, holding a full plastic cup of beer in her hand. Her leather jacket was tied around her waist, and her T-shirt, with its hippie FREE TIBET slogan, fit snugly around the chest. He wondered if she was one of those people who was always signing petitions to save whales and send famine relief to far-off countries. Because that was totally sexy. Maybe he needed a girl who wasn't self-absorbed, like Callie. And Tinsley.

"Usually someone throws up when this much alcohol is involved, so I think we did okay." Brandon had had a few too many cups of beer himself, and his tongue felt heavy in his mouth. Heath had been running around in his girl shirt, poking people and telling them to drink up since he needed to get the deposits back on the kegs. But yeah. The game of I Never had sort of spiraled out of control. He'd felt bad for Jenny—she was so sweet, it felt horrible to see her crushed in front of everyone. Another reason to despise Easy, like Brandon needed any more. What was Easy doing, taking Callie out to dinner with his dad? Christ. An idiot could have told him what a horrible idea that was.

"I like your shirt," Brandon spoke up, because he couldn't think of anything else to say. "Do you save whales too?"

"When I don't have too much homework," she replied, running her hand along the banister.

Brandon smiled. This girl was pretty sassy, which was kind of fun. If he weren't a little drunk, he'd have tried to be more witty. He wished he didn't have to struggle so much to think of something to say—but he just kept thinking about the beauty mark on her left cheek.

"Um . . . do you want to see the tunnels?" Brandon asked at last.

"The famous tunnels?" Elizabeth's eyes lit up. "I'd love to."

"Cool." Brandon started down the stairs, his legs moving slowly. Elizabeth followed him to the storage room, where the tunnel door was wide open.

"This is like the Underground Railroad—how cool!" she whispered, clearly in awe.

Brandon pulled his flashlight from his pocket and flicked it on. Immediately Elizabeth put her hand on his. "They didn't have flashlights in the Underground Railroad days—shut it off." She stepped inside the darkened tunnel, carefully making her way down the steps and disappearing into the darkness.

"Uh, wait." Brandon followed awkwardly. "Didn't they have candles in those days? They definitely had something." His sneakers hit the concrete floor of the tunnel and he squinted into the darkness.

A tiny flame burst through the darkness, illuminating Elizabeth's face, and an orb of light surrounded her. "Not Zippos, exactly. But it'll do." If possible, her face was even prettier in the wavering light coming from her lighter.

"Where do you want to go?" Brandon asked. He noticed that they were both speaking kind of softly, as their words seemed to echo in the vast, silent tunnels. It was much cooler down here with Elizabeth than it had been with all his goony guy friends.

Surprise, surprise.

Elizabeth glanced at the concrete ceiling and took a sip from her beer. "I left my Vespa in the bushes by that gatehouse or whatever it was. You know, that crumbly building at the front of campus? We could head in that direction." She held out her cup to Brandon. "Want some?"

Brandon took the cup as images of Audrey Hepburn from *Roman Holiday* flashed through his brain, wiping out thoughts of germ-swapping. He sipped her beer. "A Vespa?"

"What, is that too hipster for you, Armani?" She slyly tweaked his sweater. How'd she know it was Armani?

"Actually, I thought you'd drive a hybrid—but the leather motorcycle jacket threw me off."

Elizabeth leaned in. "Don't be disgusted," she whispered, "but it's *pleather*."

Brandon grinned. He liked that this girl was someone outside the whole incestuous Waverly in crowd. Even if she had a thing with Jeremiah, who had a thing with Brett, who . . . Brandon shook those confusing thoughts out of his head. "How'd you know Jeremiah was even here?"

She looked a little embarrassed and clicked the top back down on her Zippo, plunging them into darkness. "I'm not, like, a stalker." Silence. "He told me."

"So . . . you guys aren't together now, are you?" Somehow it was easier to ask about this in the dark. The light from the open door in the Dumbarton storage room was far behind them now, and it took Brandon's eyes a minute to adjust to the new level of darkness and be able to find the outline of Elizabeth.

"No!" Her reply came quickly, and Brandon calmed down a little. "It wasn't like that, anyway." The two of them walked forward, as if they knew where they were going. "We were just really close, you know? And then she—Brett—broke his heart. And then I guess we both got really caught up in the emotions of it all, even though it wasn't exactly about us."

"You don't have to tell me all this, you know," Brandon said, although he was psyched to hear she wasn't pining over Jeremiah. Because if strapping, broad-shouldered football players were her thing, Brandon wasn't going to have much luck.

"I know." The Zippo flicked open again, bathing Elizabeth's face in its warm glow. "I just kind of wanted to . . . clear things up."

Brandon's heart pounded.

"Anyway," she continued, tracing her empty hand against the wall. "I really came to sort of check Brett out—make sure she wasn't just toying with him again." Elizabeth paused. "Unfortunately, I think I might have fucked everything up for him."

"That's not your fault."

"Well, I didn't have to be honest—it's not like playing I Never means you're *under oath* or anything. Then maybe he could have lied, and . . ."

"I don't think that would've helped. He would've had to tell her the truth sometime." Suddenly Brandon realized he didn't exactly want to be talking about Jeremiah and Brett anymore—they would figure things out.

What he wanted to do was kiss this girl.

"And what about you? And that Jenny girl?" Elizabeth asked coyly. "You jumped up really quickly after she left, like you wanted to run out after her."

He did? Brandon didn't even remember that. "Well, she's cool. I mean, she's a friend." And it burned him up that Easy would fuck around with her too, not that it surprised him. That kid had no scruples—if he wanted Jenny one week, he got Jenny. If he wanted Callie the next, well, he'd just try and get her too. "I just, you know, felt bad for her. Her boyfriend's a dick."

"So I don't have anyone to be jealous of?"

Jealous of? Right. Like Brandon could keep his mind on anything besides how he was alone in a dark tunnel with this exciting girl in a pleather jacket and funky hair who made him feel so totally uninhibited. "I don't want to talk about other people anymore," Brandon said, taking another gulp of Elizabeth's beer as if it were some sort of electrolyte-enhanced power drink.

"Oh?" Elizabeth raised her right eyebrow as she played with her lighter, closing it and opening it and closing it again. She kept it closed. "What do you want to talk about?"

Brandon put the beer down on the floor and stepped toward where he thought Elizabeth was. It wasn't too hard to find her. He smiled in the darkness, sensing that her face was only a few inches from his. "I don't know . . . nuclear war?"

He heard her giggle, and as her mouth opened to say something, he kissed her. She kissed back eagerly, and all Brandon could think was how different and exciting it felt. His hands slid around to her lower back. He didn't even notice how dark it was because his eyes were closed.

A WAVERLY OWL ALWAYS TELLS THE TRUTH, EXCEPT WHEN IT'S WISER NOT TO.

Jenny felt like a drama queen running out of the common room the way she had, but she couldn't help it. She would have suffocated if she'd stayed in there one second longer—with Easy, who had lied to her. And with the rest of them, all staring and smirking and making her feel like such a moron for thinking that Easy could be in love with her. Why did all this have to happen? Couldn't anything ever be simple?

Because really—why would Easy take Callie out to dinner with his father if he was in love with her? It didn't make any sense. Was he ashamed of her? That she was too short? Too young? Too New York for his father? Only Callie, with her perfect blond hair and southern pedigree, was good enough?

Once she was back in her room, Jenny felt a tiny bit better. At least everyone wasn't staring at her now. And at least she didn't have to face Tinsley, who must really hate her if she was so eager to embarrass her in front of all her friends. Or maybe they weren't her friends, Jenny thought glumly as she turned on her stereo. Her palms had stopped sweating, although she still kind of felt like she might vomit at any second.

There was a light knock at the half-closed door—Easy? But Kara poked her head in. "Can I come in? Do you want some company?"

Jenny was actually kind of glad it wasn't Easy—she wasn't in the mood to talk to him, not really. Not if he couldn't tell her it was all untrue, he'd never taken Callie out to dinner. Then maybe she'd listen. But since that wasn't going to happen, Jenny wanted to figure some things out for herself first. "You can come in, if you don't mind me changing into my comfort clothes."

Kara let out a low whistle and sat down on Callie's bed. Jenny pulled her flannel Calvin Klein pajama bottoms and black tank top from her top drawer. "Tinsley certainly has a way with words, doesn't she?"

Jenny almost laughed as she took off Verena's strapless dress and her boob-crushing bra. She quickly pulled on the black tank top and her cozy pajama bottoms. There was something about flannel that was so comforting, even if the gray plaid pants were almost completely worn out at the knees. "You can say that again. It's like she gets off on humiliating other people."

Kara tucked her feet up underneath her. "You shouldn't feel humiliated. Who cares what everyone else thinks?"

"I guess I don't—I just really don't have any clue what Easy is thinking, which is the real problem. I mean, am I missing something? Why would he take Callie out to dinner?" She plopped herself down on her bed and hugged her pillow to her chest. "And not tell me about it?"

"Maybe you shouldn't overreact. Or at least, not until you talk to him. Let him explain himself. Maybe he's got a great explanation—like, he hates his dad and couldn't bear to subject you to him." Kara shrugged. "And because he doesn't really like Callie, he didn't mind taking her."

Jenny laughed dryly. "Right. Except I'm starting to think that the problem is maybe that he likes Callie too much."

"He's crazy about you," Kara insisted.

There was another gentle knock on the door. Callie pushed it open all the way, hesitantly, like she wasn't sure if she was going to get something thrown at her. Immediately Jenny softened—it really wasn't Callie's fault, any of this. Except maybe the going out with Easy in the first place part, and no one could really blame her for that. "It's okay—you can come in. I'm not mad." But the sight of Callie in the doorway—so skinny and elegant and gorgeous—made her voice quaver a little. Like she was about to burst into tears.

"Jenny, I'm so sorry." Callie rushed over toward her, looking like she kind of wanted to give her a hug but didn't know how to, exactly. "I didn't . . . want you to find out like that."

"It's okay. Easy was the one who should have told me, not you." Jenny shrugged. She felt like a kid in her black tank top, with her tiny shoulders and baggy flannel pants. "And it's not your fault Tinsley's a giant bitch."

Callie bit her lip. "I really don't know why she's like that. Maybe it's like a PMS thing."

"I've never met anyone before who has PMS twenty-four/seven," Kara put in.

Jenny shot Kara a pleading look and moved over toward the end of her bed to make more room for Callie, who was still standing in front of her. "So . . ." Her voice trailed off. She took a deep breath. "So, did anything, um . . . happen at dinner? With Easy?"

"No!" Callie replied vehemently. "It was just totally a friend thing. Things are weird with his dad, you know." She shrugged her thin shoulders. "I think it was just easier because I already knew him."

Kara gave Jenny a smile that seemed to say "I told you so." Jenny smiled kind of weakly. It didn't really make her feel much better. Callie was always going to have known Easy for longer than she had—there was no way to get around that unless she figured out a way to reverse time. It just didn't seem fair.

One look at Jenny's face and Callie could see she was already on the verge of a breakdown. No need to mention their in-the-closet hook-up. What would be the point of telling her something that would upset her even more? Something she didn't ever have to know about?

Callie tried to sound natural. "Tinsley was just . . . being a bitch. She always wants to cause as much trouble as possible, you know?" She hoped she wasn't asking for bad karma by lying again. But really. It would have been cruel to tell Jenny about the kiss.

"I'd say she succeeded." Brett flounced into the room, eyes all red and puffy. Her hair looked stringy, like she'd been running her hands through it over and over. She threw herself down on Jenny's bed. Jenny put her hand on Brett's shoulder, making Callie realize how much she missed having actual friends. Not like Tinsley, who only seemed to want to hurt people, or like Benny, who just wanted the juicy gossip.

"Are you okay, Brett?" Kara asked with concern. She was still wearing her party clothes—a romantic-looking blouse and dark flared pants. Cool clothes.

"I'll live. For now." Brett kicked off her shoes and they clunked against the floor. "But if you guys are talking about how much guys suck, it would definitely be helpful."

"Did you really throw a drink in Heath's face?" Callie asked Kara abruptly.

"Only because he really, really deserved it," she replied. "He's such a skeeze. He was a complete asshole to me for an entire year, and now that I'm—whatever, not fat anymore—he thinks he can just turn on the charm and I'll fall all over him?" Kara's cheeks were pink with irritation.

Callie nodded slowly, not really understanding. Someone was going to have to fill her in. But throwing a beer at Heath was pretty funny. Heath always seemed to get everything handed to him on a silver platter—from grades he didn't work for to girls he didn't deserve. About time someone threw it back in his face. "Do all guys have such short-term memories?" She was, of course, thinking of Easy as she said this. Had he forgotten that he'd dumped her? That he'd had her for a whole year and then decided he didn't want her anymore? And then two weeks later, thought, What the hell? I might as well take her out to dinner, and kiss her, and Jenny who? Grr. It wasn't right to treat anyone that way, and Callie felt stupid for letting it go so far. "Is it, like, a testosterone thing?"

"You mean, testosterone makes them think with their penises?" Brett sat up in bed. "Well, that's completely obnoxious. It's not like we think with our ovaries." Her hands were gripped into little fists. In fact, she looked even angrier than when she'd stormed out of the party.

"Let's not talk about reproductive organs," Callie piped up. "It makes me a little squeamish."

"Penis. Testes. Fallopian tubes. Uterus," Kara barked out quickly as Callie pressed her hands to her ears. Everyone burst out laughing, even Jenny and Brett, who'd been looking like death.

"Can't we just agree that all guys are jerks? At least sometimes?" Callie rubbed the back of her neck, which was all in knots after the long stressful evening.

"Guys only act like jerks when someone lets them," Kara pointed out, tracing her finger along Callie's quilted bedspread. "What if every girl just agreed to stop letting them get away with it?"

"Then they'd have to learn to behave like human beings." Brett twirled a lock of fiery red hair around her finger.

"Let's make a pact," Callie suggested, suddenly interested in doing something to ensure that she wasn't going to let Easy jerk her around anymore.

"Okay," Jenny said quickly, from out of her long silence. "How about we all agree to respect ourselves so guys will respect us?" She bit her lip. "I mean, if we all do the first part, the second part will just . . . happen."

"Maybe we can work it into the responsible Owl essay," Brett suggested, tapping her chin with her peach-polished finger. "You know, a responsible Owl doesn't let boys push her around, et cetera. It can be kind of a girl power thing."

"Do you think we can all hand in the same one?" Kara asked hopefully. "I mean, they probably saw *The Breakfast Club* in theaters when it came out. Giving us a collective detention is sort of, like, asking for it."

"It could be kind of symbolic—like we have only one answer because . . ." Jenny gave a sheepish grin and paused. "We're kind of all the same, you know, *underneath*."

Right. As ridiculous as that sounded, and it sounded pretty ridiculous, the girls glanced around at each other and considered how true it was. Jenny, in her pajamas, with her dark curls pulled into a messy knot at the back of her head. Brett, her eyes bleary but determined. Kara, who was almost a complete stranger, with her enormous greenish brown eyes taking in the scene, her cheeks flushed like she was actually excited about this whole weekend. And Callie—well, for once, she didn't care what she looked like. All she knew was that this felt kind of nice.

"A pact," Callie repeated.

Grinning like they meant it, the four of them leaned forward and put their hands in a pile, like they were getting ready to do a field hockey cheer. It was kind of hokey, but like a cheer, it made Callie feel, at least for a moment, that she was really part of something. That maybe she wasn't so alone anymore.

A RESPONSIBLE OWL KNOWS HOW TO KEEP A SECRET—ESPECIALLY IF IT MEANS HE GETS TO KEEP THE GIRL.

"I can't believe Heath and I dragged a keg up here!" Julian exclaimed. He was standing at the edge of the roof, looking over the stone wall and down at the wrought iron fire escape.

"A half keg," Tinsley pointed out teasingly from behind him. "And why'd you do that, again?"

"A pretty girl told me to." Julian picked up a pebble from the gravelly roof, blew on it, and swung his arm back and forth a few times before flinging it out over the quad below, like he was skimming a stone across a pond.

"Do you do everything pretty girls tell you to do?"

"What can I say? I was raised right."

He was certainly doing *something* right. After the party disbanded, Julian and Tinsley and a few others had wandered upstairs to the smaller common room that housed the TV and DVD player. Julian, a little shyly, had pulled from his messenger bag the library's copy of *Rosencrantz and Guildenstern Are Dead*. "Since your film meeting had to be postponed," he'd whispered. Tinsley, at that moment, was thankful they weren't alone—otherwise, who knows what would have happened. Instead, while Lon and Benny snuggled up on the chintz love seat, the two of them sat a comfortable distance away from each other on the oversized sofa. Which sagged in the middle, meaning that they were slowly sliding toward each other, and at the beginning of each scene Tinsley had to move away or else she'd end up in his lap.

Not that she would have had a problem with that if they had been alone. But . . . there were a lot of factors to consider. She knew it was silly—age shouldn't matter. Madonna was ten years older than Guy Ritchie! But Guy Ritchie wasn't a freshman.

It really was more than that, though. Her favorite moments were the ones leading up to that first kiss—when you're not sure if it's going to happen or what it's going to feel like, when your nerves are all on edge, waiting for it. Sometimes—sadly, too many times, for Tinsley—the anticipation was better than the payoff. The kiss, and the guy, often disappointed her. And once the kiss was over and it was only so-so, the whole thing basically ended.

And she really didn't want that to happen with Julian. It felt so thrilling to be sitting next to him in the dark, with Benny and Lon just a few feet away, watching one of the funniest movies on earth and trying not to wonder what Julian's lips would taste like. He had a great laugh, too—like he didn't care who was listening.

After the credits rolled, they snuck out of the common room, Benny's head lying softly against Lon's big chest, one of them snoring loudly, and snuck up to the roof. Where they were now.

"Come here," Julian said suddenly, looking down over the edge again. Tinsley quickly approached him and peeked over, wondering if Pardee was finally coming home. But she didn't see anything except the dark grass and bushes far below. Nothing even moved.

"What am I supposed to be looking at?" Tinsley demanded, aware of how close she was standing to Julian. He was only inches away.

"Oh, I don't know."

Tinsley looked up at him, puzzled. He'd taken off his knit cap at some point in the night, and the breeze ruffled his grungy hair. The dimple at the corner of his lips deepened. "I just wanted you to come closer."

"Oh," Tinsley replied. "What else do you want?" A shiver ran through her body.

"I want you to stop asking questions so I can kiss you."

"Why would you . . ." she started, suddenly feeling nervous that things were happening too quickly. She didn't know if she was ready to give up that anticipation yet. But then Julian leaned toward her and pressed his lips to her right cheek, holding them there for a moment, and Tinsley remembered what his hair smelled like—pine trees.

He hadn't said anything to her about the bitchy way she'd ended the stupid game of I Never, and Tinsley liked that. He didn't seem surprised, or disappointed, or anything—he just seemed to like her.

And so she couldn't help herself any longer. She let her nose brush against his, and then her lips touched his, gently and then harder, and Julian's hands tightened around her waist as he pulled her toward him.

He may be young, but he definitely knows how to kiss, she thought.

"See?" Tinsley said when she pulled away from him, but not too far. "I know how to shut up sometimes."

Julian pushed back her hair and kissed her ear, or kind of kissed it, his soft lips actually just touching it lightly. Then his mouth slid down to her neck, sending an icy explosion of pleasure through her body. "Don't get me wrong, I like it when you talk too. . . ." His words felt even more intimate than kisses against her skin. "But it's nice to mix things up. I really dig you, you know."

Tinsley sighed. "You hardly know me." She pulled herself out of his arms and leaned against the wall around the roof.

"I don't know about that," Julian countered. "I know how you shave your legs in the shower. I know how you start to giggle even before a funny line comes in a movie just because you know it's coming. I know you have a funny little mole behind your left ear that only really lucky people get to see. Or to kiss."

Tinsley stared at the multitude of stars in the sky, which

seemed to be winking at her. "Thanks," she said dreamily, wishing they could both fall asleep up here. "I like you too."

Julian ran a hand through his hair, making it all flop over to one side. He looked kind of like one of those starving rock stars. He could use a little meat on his bones. Tinsley picked up a pack of cloves that someone—Callie?—must have left up there, a box of matches next to it. She lit one up and offered the box to Julian. He shook his head. "No one is going to believe this." He had a kind of goofy grin slapped on his face.

"Wait, what?" Tinsley was suddenly wide awake. "We can't actually tell people about this. This has to be, kind of, our secret."

Julian looked like she'd just thrown a bucked of cold water on him. "Why?"

Because you're a freshman, she wanted to cry. But instead she gathered her thoughts and spoke calmly, like she was presenting her position in a debate—except this was definitely not debatable. "I don't mean it in a bad way—but you haven't been here long, so you haven't seen how all Waverly relationships tend to crash and burn under all the intense scrutiny." She shrugged innocently, but she was already thinking about Jenny and Easy's imminent collapse. "I just don't want that to happen to . . . this, you know?"

"It's not that you're afraid of dating a freshman, is it?" Julian's brown eyes examined her face, as if searching for clues.

"Not one as hot as you," she replied quickly. The freshman thing really was only part of it. In reality, Tinsley was just kind of . . . bad . . . at relationships. As soon as she felt like she was in one, she wanted out. And the prying eyes of Waverly Owls did nothing to help the situation. As soon as it was rumored that two people were dating, people always seemed astonished to see them apart. Tinsley hated the thought of people greeting her with "Where's Julian?" It was like once you were a couple, you ceased to exist as an individual. It made her a little sick to her stomach.

And right now, her feelings for Julian were just so pleasant, she didn't want to fuck it up.

"It'll be so much cooler if it's just between us," she continued, seeing that Julian was wavering. "There'll be no one to get in the way."

"Does anyone ever say no to you?" Julian asked after a short pause. His eyes twinkled with exasperation, like he knew he was getting into something he should resist but couldn't.

"Rarely," she admitted, her mouth curling into a grin.

From: BrettMesserschmidt@waverly.edu
To: DeanMarymount@waverly.edu
CC: KathrynRose@waverly.edu, Dumbarton residents
Date: Sunday, October 6, 5:14 p.m.
Subject: Essay

Dear Dean Marymount and Miss Rose,

We accept the fact that we had to sacrifice an entire weekend in lock-down for what we did. What we did WAS wrong. But we have come to a different conclusion after discussing what we think a responsible Owl is. You see Waverly Owls as you want to see Waverly Owls—in the simplest terms and the most convenient definitions. You see us as legacies, princesses, psych cases, delinquents, band geeks, and responsible Owls. Correct? That's the way we saw each other before we were locked in. We were brainwashed.

We are not all guilty of what you thought we were—but we are all guilty of something. We are guilty of giving in to labels, to letting them be placed on ourselves, and for trying to fill them.

Therefore, it has come to our collective realization that a "responsible Owl"

Does not try to be someone she is not, even when wearing someone else's clothes

Knows who her dormmates are and who they are not

Does not lie about herself, to others or to herself

Says what she means and means what she says

Respects herself so that others will too

Email Inbox

This is our collective answer. This is what we have learned this weekend and what we won't forget.

Sincerely,

The Girls of Dumbarton

Instant Message Inbox

BennyCunningham: Nice work, B! I'm proud to call you my class prefect. How'd you come up with all that crap?

BrettMesserschmidt: Jenny and Callie and Kara helped me. And I'm not convinced it's crap . . .

BennyCunningham: You mean J and C haven't strangled each other yet??

BrettMesserschmidt: I don't think that's going to happen—at least, not anymore.

BennyCunningham: Everybody's talking about Kara throwing her beer in Heath's face—that was pretty effing cool. . . . She's a funky chick. I'm glad we got to discover her.

BrettMesserschmidt: She's been downstairs all year, B. . . . It's not like she was waiting for you to discover her or anything.

BennyCunningham: Still . . . I like her style. She's got . . . I don't know. Something.

BrettMesserschmidt: Maybe we all do.

FOUR BEST FRIENDS. FOUR HIGH SCHOOL DIPLOMAS.

ONE BOMBSHELL ANNOUNCEMENT THAT CHANGES EVERYTHING.

Harper Waddle, Sophie Bushell, and Kate Foster are about to commit the ultimate suburban sin—bailing on college to pursue their dreams. Middlebury-bound Becca Winsberg is convinced her friends have gone insane . . . until they remind her she just might have a dream of her own. So what if their lives are bass ackwards and belly up? They'll always have each other.

BASS ACKWARDS AND BELLY UP

AVAILABLE NOW